A Promise Made

A Novel by
Clifton LaBree

Published by
Fading Shadows Imprint
New Boston, New Hampshire

ISBN-10:1943329028
ISBN-13:978-1-943329-02-1

Cover Design by Vivian LaBree

Dedicated to my wife Pauline, and my family, with thanks for all their support and encouragement.

Chapter One

(January 1945, A Japanese Prison Compound North of Manila on Luzon Island.)

A suffocating hot breeze passed through the darkened prison compound. The aroma of unwashed bodies and open wounds festered with maggots and gangrene filled the air. It was the smell of death so strong it was almost smothering. The huts where the emaciated skeleton-like American soldiers slept on their bamboo mats placed on the ground were permeated with the stench of death. The humid temperatures of the tropics only intensified the odors. When the wind changed direction it swept over the open latrine ditches adding to the symphony of putridness the inmates had to contend with.

Some of the inmates became nauseous and vomited even though their sense of smell had been repeatedly assaulted and violated by the deteriorating conditions that existed in the Japanese compound for American prisoners. The fetid smells were a normal part of their daily lives.

Captain Jack Ross of the United States Army rested on the bamboo mat he had recently woven out of fresh stalks from the nearby jungle. He listened to the sounds of the night when nocturnal animals rose from their daylight slumber and took over the landscape, contributing to the loud cacophony rising from the dark, menacing countryside. Birds and animals called to each other in staggered cadences interrupted by shrieks from some unfortunate creature being attacked and consumed. The law of the jungle, survival of the fittest, was well understood by the inmates.

Just before dusk, Captain Ross had tried to comfort Sergeant Edward Buxton, a tall lanky farmer from northern Maine with the heart of a lion and the soul of a saint. Buxton had worked feverishly for the welfare of his men. Eighteen men from his company, along with hundreds of American soldiers, had surrendered with him at Bataan on April 9, 1942. Five were lost in the long agonizing sixty-five mile march out of the Bataan peninsula to the north where they were loaded on cattle cars and shipped by rail to a compound surrounded by swamps and jungles in the foothills of the Sierra Madre Mountains north of Manila. Escape was all but impossible. The inmates had facetiously nicknamed the compound *Hotel Utopia*.

The first accurate inventory the officers were able to conduct since the surrender of forces at Bataan, took place the day they arrived at the compound. The Japanese were indifferent to their roster of occupants. All they wanted to know was the number of prisoners. Several men were lost in the suffocating cattle cars where they were packed so tightly that the dead men remained standing for the duration of the trip. They were left behind on the feces-covered floor of the cars when the inmates reached their destination. The living were suffering from exhaustion, starvation, multiple wounds, and diseases endemic to the tropics. The trek to the north had depleted their ranks by fifty percent!

Captain Ross and Sergeant Buxton had worked tirelessly during the months of captivity to maintain the morale of the men, but the long hours of forced labor and insufficient nutrition had taken the lives of five men in their company. The remaining survivors were walking skeletons with large heads and shrunken bodies.

Three days after the vicious beating of Sergeant Buxton, Jack knew that the intrepid sergeant had arrived at a point where death was preferable to living. It came in the middle of the night when the Sergeant Buxton cried out in a weak tremulous voice to his betrothed Joyce. The cry ended in a raspy gurgle. He had passed over to eternity, free of pain and suffering!

Jack had seen the same thing, almost on a daily basis, since they had occupied the prison compound. The men simply willed themselves to die when all hope was lost. Jack had to fight the same impulse on several occasions. Death had to be better than the existence they endured with no specific knowledge that any of them would be spared or liberated. After three long years of never hearing a word from the outside world about the conduct of the war, hope became a scarce virtue, a fantasy without foundation.

The death of Sergeant Buxton passed without mourning. Jack accepted the reality of his death. It was easy because death was a constant companion. His only worry was that he might not have the physical strength to transport the ninety-pound body to the burial area. Burial details took place every day, first thing in the morning, before the sun climbed too high in the sky. Lately, the numbers of dead bodies had increased, and the live inmates were pushed to the limits of their strength digging the graves to bury their comrades.

Those who died in their sleep had a relaxed expression of newly found peace. It was in stark contrast to the agony of long days working in the fields without sustenance and the incessant brutality of the prison guards that brought the men to death's doorstep. The moment of their passage from the squalor of the compound to a new spiritual dimension was one of peaceful release welcomed by every death Jack had witnessed.

Tepid rice soup was their daily food ration. They were steadily starving to death. A few desperate souls had resorted to the revolting spectacle of eating the maggots that crawled over the open sores and wounds of their comrades. If one had the stomach for it, it was a rich source of protein, but very few had a strong enough constitution to partake of that kind of nourishment. The starvation diet was directly responsible for scurvy, beriberi, and amebic dysentery that were epidemic throughout the compound. Wounds to the arms or legs that failed to heal properly were frequently followed by painful and crude amputation of infected limbs by the surviving members in each hut. There were no doctors or medics left in the

3

compound and the Japanese were indifferent to their medical needs. During the second year of confinement, large numbers of men lost teeth. However, the most dreaded symptom of a prolonged starvation diet was blindness. It was an affliction that was appearing with alarming frequency.

The most powerful motive for survival for Captain Ross was the memories he treasured of his beloved wife, Myla. He saw her face everywhere. In the privacy of the night he purposely willed himself to another time and place where love and peace had filled his life. He returned time and again to the small cottage he and Myla had been fixing up on the coast of Maine. His ability to escape from the heartache of the prison compound to his private sanctuary probably kept him sane and alive.

Memories of Myla were bountiful. He had fallen in love with her when he was a little boy in grade school. He first told her that he loved her at a Halloween party when they were in the seventh grade. She smiled at him and answered shyly with a girlish giggle: "I like you too, Jack, but we're only thirteen years old!" It was an incident they both remembered with clarity and tenderness as they grew older.

Wells was a small seacoast town in southern Maine filled with hard working people who supplemented their incomes whenever possible from the large influx of summer tourists that flocked to the beautiful sandy beaches. Jack's father kept busy year-round working as a self-employed house painter. Most of his income came from summer residents camps and homes along the waterfront. Isaac Ross was a small wiry man with a prominent nose and a receding hairline. He had a habit of speaking his mind and those who knew him well thought highly of his friendship. He was an energetic man with a big heart and a generous soul.

Jack loved his father for his gentle ways and patient disposition. Jack's mother had died giving him birth. He never knew the softness and joy of a mother, but his father kept her memory alive with stories of the love they had shared growing up in the small town together. Later, when Jack had graduated from college and was waiting for the train to report for duty with the Army, he had asked his father, who was well liked in the small community, why he had never married after his mother's death.

Isaac Ross looked surprised at his son's question and calmly remarked: "Well, Son, I haven't found anyone who could make me feel the way I did for your mother. I promised to love and honor her until the day I die. Without a doubt she's in Heaven now with our Lord, but she's also in my heart as strong as the day we first married. A promise made is a promise to be kept. I owe that commitment to her memory."

Jack never forgot those simple words spoken from the heart, *a promise made....* They represented a way of life that had sustained his father through years of lonely days and nights. In that moment of truth, Jack understood the strength and discipline that guided his father through the difficult years of raising a son alone. He never loved his father as much as he did at that moment of discovery, standing on the platform of the train station at Wells. It was their last farewell.

Myla and Jack attended the University of New Hampshire together, graduating in 1939. He had a degree in engineering and military science. Myla earned a degree in English and education. Immediately after graduation, he had joined the Army with a second lieutenant commission to fulfill his obligation under the Reserve Officer Training Corps (ROTC). A year later, they were wed and moved into married officer quarters at Fort Bragg, North Carolina, while Jack attended an Army command school. Myla took a teaching job at the base school to help out with finances. They were able to spend most evenings and weekends together. It was a happy time for them.

They had purchased a small seasonal cottage on the rocky Maine coast between Kennebunkport and Wells. The building was unsuitable for year-round use without additional insulation and repairs. Located on a bluff overlooking the ocean from three directions, they were drawn to its charm. There was a peaceful energy about the place that captivated both of them. It felt like home even before they signed for its purchase. With both of their paychecks combined, the cottage and necessary remodeling expenses were within their financial means.

There were ominous signs of potential war on the horizon. The Japanese were expanding their empire and influence into Manchuria, and Germany was rampaging through Europe meeting little or no resistance. The world was tense about the future. The United States was declared a neutral nation but the U.S. Navy and Coast Guard were escorting supply transports across the Atlantic to England, and American troops were stationed in Iceland at the request of the British Commonwealth. Jack firmly insisted that the title to the cottage be in Myla's name instead of joint custody. A war was inevitable, and he did not want any complications for Myla in case something happened to him. He had heard the beat of distant drums!

On October 20, 1941, Jack's company received orders for duty in the Philippines. When he left, Myla returned to live at the cottage. He was promoted to the rank of first lieutenant as the company's executive officer. That night, Myla replaced his gold second lieutenant bar with a silver one. It was the last night they spent together. Myla was brave and put on a positive front. Her soldier-husband was going half-way around the world at a time when it was beginning to come apart. Fear and apprehension were a natural part of a soldier's wife. Tears came easy that evening. Their good-bye was passionate, intense, and heartfelt.

Jack relived their last evening minute by minute. The memory gave him the courage to resist the temptation to lie down and just fade away to oblivion. His Myla deserved better, so he suffered the daily beatings and criminal brutality of the Japanese in silence. The guards were rotated occasionally over the years. Each new group of soldiers exhibited the same cruel and sadistic desires to inflict pain on the prisoners. The unyielding behavior and low intelligence of each group of replacements seemed to be a common description of compound guards. Slapping and physical assault of Japanese soldiers by their superiors was a frequent occurrence. The more inept soldiers at the bottom of the pecking order were recipients of most of the abuse. When they had the opportunity to express dominance and superiority over the prisoners in their charge, they took great delight in lashing out with cruel, vindictive behavior. It made the guards feel superior. The inmates were looked upon as the lowest of human beings. They had chosen to surrender when the Japanese would have preferred death by their own hand instead of incarceration by an enemy. The hatred that existed between the captors and tormentors was a motivating force that helped sustain the prisoners. Some day the inmates would have their revenge, and that miniscule hope strengthened them.

The inhumane treatment over a prolonged period of time was capable of turning every man into a robotic skeleton, but the morale of the prisoners remained exceedingly high with few exceptions. Some were driven to madness and died or were killed by the guards. They proudly and defiantly stood up to the malicious conduct of the Japanese and symbolically spit in their face. Occasionally, there was an incident that bolstered the prisoner's pride and brought a few chuckles to their dreary existence.

None of the Japanese spoke English except for their camp commandant. One of the guards usually stationed near the main gate took great delight in stabbing any inmate that came close to him with his bayonet. He pricked them just enough to draw blood. One day Sergeant Buxton received several jabs from the smiling guard who thought it was great sport. Buxton cried out in pain calling the guard an "asshole". The guard did not understand what was being said and gestured menacingly at the injured Buxton. He thought for sure that he was going to be bayoneted, and screamed in a loud voice "...asshole, asshole..." and pointed to the Japanese flag with the large red rising sun flying on the main gate pole. The guard did not understand at first. Buxton repeated the words and gestured vigorously until the guard misinterpreted his meaning and smiled proudly. He saluted the flag several times as he repeated the words "asshole... asshole...."

Every day Sergeant Buxton, Jack, and others, who knew about the ruse, greeted the guard bowing solemnly to the flag while repeating the epitaph over and over. It increased morale in the camp one hundred percent for the few days the joke worked. The Commandant eventually found out about the trick played on the simple-minded guard and had him replaced. Sergeant Buxton was singled out for one of the most brutal beatings meted out by the Japanese. They repeatedly smashed every inch of his body with rifle butts, breaking his shoulder and two wrists. His left ear was hanging by a slender thread of flesh. Sergeant Buxton suffered greatly and deteriorated rapidly after the beating. There was no doctor in the compound and no medical supplies or facilities to treat diseases or injuries. Jack did his best to make the courageous sergeant as comfortable as possible. It would have been cruel to deny him the comfort of death.

The day they heard artillery gunfire in the distance for the first time, a two-engine fighter-bomber, one soldier recognized it as an American B-25, buzzed the compound spraying the four corner guard towers with machine and cannon fire from the nose of the aircraft. Two of the towers were obliterated. The inmates huddled in their shacks silently cheering. The plane banked in a tight circle and made a slow run directly over the open assembly area barely clearing the top of the surrounding palm trees. Suddenly thousands of small packages streamed out of the bomb bay doors beneath the aircraft. The ground around the huts was littered with packages the size of several packs of cigarettes. The inmates rushed to collect the packages shouting and waving at the plane. The guards were still numbed by the suddenness of the attack, leaving the inmates free to collect most of the packages and run back to their huts without interference.

The packets were life-saving treasures containing cigarettes, matches, candy bars, chewing gum, a pencil with a small pad of paper and a small sewing kit. The inmates later learned that they were called "Victory Packages". General MacArthur's staff conceived the idea to keep hope alive within the occupied Philippine Islands. The outer wrapping contained an American and a Filipino flag on one side and the statement "I Shall Return" in bold letters on the other. They were widely distributed throughout the islands by aircraft and submarines that rose out of the water in safe lagoons to discharge their freight and pick up rescued airmen. The packages raised the hopes of every man in the compound. Perhaps their long tenure in hell would soon be over… perhaps!

The presence of the B-25, and the muffled rumblings they could hear south of the compound, were encouraging signs to the beleaguered inmates. One day a squadron of Lockheed P-38 twin-fuselage fighters were spotted flying in formation directly overhead at a high altitude. One of the fighters peeled off and buzzed the compound several times wagging its wings in salute to the long-suffering inmates. The men waved frantically and screamed until they were hoarse. The sight of the American star on the wings of the plane filled them with pride and hope. The plane was so low that Jack could see the pilot in the cockpit. He waved back at the airman. The guards looked on with worry and fear in their eyes. The inmates knew that they were entering the most dangerous period of their incarceration. Frightened guards could become trigger happy if they felt cornered.

Throughout the years of internment, the prisoners were denied Red Cross packages and mail. Not one letter was delivered to any of the men, and none were collected by the prison administration to be sent out. The last letter he had received from Myla was posted December 17, 1941, at Wells, Maine. He had received it on Bataan early in January 1942.

For more than three years the prisoners were completely isolated from the rest of the world without mail or radio news bulletins. They worked daily in the sugar cane fields to the point of exhaustion and returned to their huts where each man groped for the bamboo mats they slept on. Without the life-giving benefits of the pilfered stalks of sugar cane, they would have perished from starvation. The rice soup was not enough to support life. Sugar cane stalks made the difference between life and death. They were prevented from raising their own vegetables. The guards claimed they had no seed available for them. The inmates would have to rely on the Japanese Army supplies. The guards did not fare much better than the prisoners and they, too, ate sugar cane stalks.

The last letter that Jack received from Myla was the only personal property he carried out of the Bataan peninsula into captivity. He had lost his helmet and dog tags two days before his regiment surrendered when a Japanese mortar round exploded beside him, peppering his backside with shrapnel. A medic removed as many of the metal pieces he could locate and treated the wounds with sulfa powder. Luckily for him, the wounds did not become infected. The tattered clothes on his back and the precious letter in his pocket were all that he possessed. The letter was severely tattered and perspiration-soiled from daily handling. He could recite its contents word for word.

Wells, Maine
December 17, 1941

My darling Husband,

I am so empty without you at my side, sweetheart. I think of you often. The news from the Philippines is not good and we are all concerned for you. I pray that my love will be your protective armor and when this horrible war is over we can start our lives anew.

I'm filling in as a substitute teacher in Kennebunk this year. It will help me pass the days while you're away. You'll be pleased to know that I've completed the painting in the bathroom. Now the house interior is finished. Your father has been a lot of help. He wants to stain the exterior cedar shingles this spring. I know that he finds comfort in keeping busy and giving of himself. You have many of his personality traits and are a lot like him.

We have finally gotten our gasoline ration cards. Our Nash Ambassador is allotted three gallons of gasoline a week, so there won't be many extra trips taken. I've had the tires rotated as you suggested and am keeping it under cover in our new garage.

I keep your picture next to my heart and send you my love and kisses often. I'm so proud of you my darling. I wait with anxious impatience for your return to my arms.

All my love,
Myla

Chapter Two

Jack was lucky compared to most of the soldiers that surrendered on Bataan. He had begun captivity sore and tender from the shrapnel wounds that hurt so much he walked in a bent over position. For some reason the Japanese guards did not view him as insolent or disobedient, and he escaped many of the random acts of murder and wanton cruelty. He attributed it to the fact that he walked as much as possible in the interior of the column of marching men instead of the outside edge where the prisoners were accessible for the sadistic guards to bayonet at random. Those who stumbled or fell from the column were instantly shot or bayoneted.

The American forces that surrendered on Bataan had held the Japanese off for three months. It was a vicious campaign of attrition. The U. S. Army could not be resupplied. Therefore, it became a medical and a supply defeat. Consumption without replenishment was not a recipe for success. Malnutrition and starvation were widespread long before the surrender took place.

Jack and Sergeant Buxton carried a badly wounded soldier from their platoon, suspended between them, the full sixty-five miles of the march. They both wept openly when the soldier died of heat exhaustion in the crowded cattle car that carried them to their final destination. There were no windows on the cattle cars. No one knew where they were being taken. They only knew that they were heading north of Bataan and Manila towards the central portions of Luzon, and they could see the peaks of the Sierra Madre Mountains located in northeastern Luzon.

Life at the prison camp was a constant struggle for survival. Jack was senior officer in one of the bamboo huts housing approximately one hundred men. He and other hut commanders had set up escape committees and began the patient job of collecting information about the surrounding area and everything they could about the guard detachment. The jungle and swamps that surrounded the prison compound looked formidable. Several acres of land had been cleared adjacent to the compound for the production of sugar cane. The general consensus of opinion was that the logical escape route from the compound should be to the south, but beyond that, nothing was known except that the railhead was within twenty miles of the prison.

The size of the guard contingent was not excessive and it varied in size. The hut commanders estimated their strength at between fifty and one hundred forty. Overpowering the guards had its own set of risks, but so did the daily work routine with limited rations. Some of the men still wore remnants of their original Army issue footgear. Those who were barefoot developed footworm and ringworm so badly they could not walk. Lack of adequate footwear was one of the most crucial factors in planning any escape. Shoe leather deteriorated rapidly in the tropics, and by the third year of internment, most of the men were going barefoot. Planning and discussing the potentials for an escape helped to occupy their minds and distract them from their daily toil, even if they knew in their hearts that an escape was next to impossible.

By March 1942, most of the men had succumbed to malaria. Quinine could control the disease but none was available to the men in the camps. The Japanese never offered any kind of medical assistance to the inmates. Their general physical condition precluded any attempted breakout. They were simply too weak to travel very far in rough unknown country, even if they could overpower the guards. The hope of finding additional foodstuff in the Japanese supply dump may have made it more feasible, but the guards assigned to the camp also seemed to be at the short end of the food chain. They ate similar rations as the inmates; however, they were able to supplement their diets with fruits, vegetables and animals from the surrounding jungle, which they did on a regular basis. They never shared their harvests from the tropical forest with their charges.

If an escape attempt were made from the camp they would need to have a Filipino with them who spoke the language. There were two Filipino scouts that accompanied them into captivity - one was in Jack's hut. He became very sick and died from what they all assumed was food poisoning. His companion was so overwhelmed by the daily work routine and meager rations that he committed suicide by attacking a guard and successfully subduing him. The Filipino scout was extremely agile and made it to the top of the barbed wire that surrounded the camp before he was riddled with machine gun fire from one of the stockade guard towers.

Every prisoner occupied his mind with escape plots. In reality, it was nearly impossible without some outside assistance, but hope was all they had left. They prayed for some contact with the native population or local guerrilla bands they knew were prevalent throughout the islands, especially in the mountain regions. The months and years went by without physical contact from anyone except the Japanese guards. Their isolation from the rest of the world made them feel as if they were the last people on the face of the earth. That began to change when they observed more and more American aircraft flying overhead.

The planes rekindled hope where it had faltered in the total isolation imposed upon them. Some inmates were lost to disease and injuries that became infected. Others were driven to madness when all hope had been drained from their consciousness. As the years rolled by, more and more men began to lose their teeth, another symptom of malnutrition. Jack had lost three teeth by late 1944. He was one of the more fortunate ones. Most had lost more than that a year ago.

One morning a few days after the B-25 bomber had dropped the victory packages into the compound, the men were roused from a sound sleep by the sudden eruption of small arms gunfire and the explosion of grenades all around the compound. Instinctively the inmates remained on the ground with their bamboo mats pulled around them afraid that the Japanese were starting to massacre the prisoners.

The men had prepared for this contingency and agreed that if they were going to die anyway, they were going to take some of the guards with them. They had planned to rush the main gate in masse recognizing that some would be killed. The rationale was that a few might survive and successfully climb the wire to freedom. Jack was rallying the men in his hut to get ready for the assault on the front gate. They gathered what few belongings each person had been able to save over the years and readied themselves for the ensuing action.

Suddenly, an announcement from a megaphone in English pierced the early morning air: "American prisoners. We are Rangers from the United States Army. Stay in your buildings until we neutralize the Japanese guards. Soon you will be free. I repeat: stay in your huts. Your deliverance is at hand. God Bless America."

It took a while for the concept of freedom to sink in. Some refused to believe that it was true. Most simply sat quietly on their bamboo mats and silently wept. All the fear and hatred they had lived with for three years began to disappear. It was replaced with an indescribable euphoria and pride in once again being an American soldier. All had resigned themselves to the fact that they would perish in this God forsaken hellhole, never to know their families and loved ones again. Now, hope was rekindled.

Physical weakness and lack of endurance limited what they could do to assist the Rangers in eliminating the enemy. They were resigned to wait quietly as they had been requested to do. Jack had secretly accumulated two nails about four inches long from the scrap lumber once used to repair the building. Over several months he had fashioned bamboo sections to each end of the nails to act as a handle. It was crude and fragile, but he would be able to inflict some damage to a Japanese guard if and when he was forced to defend himself. He had sharpened the pointed ends of the nails on rocks by honing them for hours at a time in the darkness of the hut. Now they were sharp as needles. Each night he fondled them and dreamed of a chance to strike back.

None of the prisoners were physically capable of overpowering the guards. It was even doubtful if two or three prisoners could do the job. Therefore, each inmate had tried to fashion some kind of a weapon as an equalizer to their fragile physical condition. Whatever they lacked in strength they made up for in determination and courage to attempt the unthinkable. Each in their own way had reached the point where they believed it was inevitable that they would die in the camp, but the enemy would pay some price. A quick death was preferable to a slow lingering one which had been their lot for the past three years.

The prisoners were concentrated at the interior wall of the building furthest from the flashes of gunfire and the flurry of rushing men. The hut was still dark inside and the prisoners watched the two entrances wondering what was taking place outside. Jack knew that the four guard towers would be the first structures a rescue force would destroy. The intensity of gunfire and explosions were greatest at the towers and the main entrance gate where the Japanese quarters were located.

A short burst from a Thompson sub-machine gun at one of their openings quickened the pulse of the inmates. A Japanese guard, the same one who had beaten Sergeant Buxton, sought refuge within the darkness of the hut. Jack was the closest to the guard who was occupied with adjusting to the blackness inside and unaware of Jack's presence. The wary guard looked back at the entrance of the hut to see if he had been followed.

It was the opportunity Jack had long been waiting for. He lunged at the guard with a speed that surprised him. The guard was holding his rifle at the ready with both hands in case someone followed him through the door. Jack came at him from behind with the two sharpened nails, one in each outstretched hand. With all the strength he could muster, Jack drove the nails into the unsuspecting guard's ears with a rapid motion as if he was clapping his hands together. Both nails penetrated the skull to their full depth. The Japanese soldier emitted a high pitched scream and dropped his rifle reaching for the deadly weapons that had penetrated his brain. Jack pulled the nails from his head and repeated the movement. Their figures were silhouetted against the lightened entranceway so that the inmates could see what had happened. They immediately leaped upon the guard pounding and kicking him with all the strength they possessed. They felt good repaying some of the brutality they had received. Jack screamed for them to stop when it was evident that the soldier was dead, but the inmates continued to pound on the body until it was a lifeless lump of bleeding flesh. They had drawn blood and were elated with the results.

Several American Rangers appeared at the entrance asking the inmates to come out of their huts. The compound had been cleared. Jack walked through the entrance and spoke to the Rangers.

"I'm Captain Jack Ross, commander of this building," he stated. "The men are coming out as you request. Okay, gang, you heard the Rangers, come on out to meet our rescue team. Remember, we're still soldiers even if we don't look much like soldiers."

One hundred prisoners stepped out into the burning brilliance of the sun holding their claw-like hands over their eyes for protection. Four sturdy American Rangers watched the men file out of the hut with dropped jaws and a lump in their throats. The inmates were nothing but skin and bones with tattered remnants of clothing partially covering their emaciated bodies. The Rangers had expected to find them thin and undernourished, but the men before them had passed that point a long time ago. The forlorn look of lost hope and familiarity of death shown in deep-set eyes that looked the Rangers over from top to bottom. The eyes moved the Rangers the most. One of them was so touched by their pitiful condition that he wept with them.

"Which one of you is Captain Ross?" asked a burly Ranger sergeant, holding a Thompson sub-machine gun as if it was a toy.

"I'm Captain Ross," Jack announced, stepping before the sergeant. Jack felt ashamed and self-conscious of the pitiful sight he must have presented to the Ranger commander. "I apologize for the way we look, Sergeant. It's been a long time...." Jack was filled with emotion. His body shook and a mist covered his sunken bloodshot eyes. Words failed him.

The Ranger sergeant reached out and embraced the emotional Captain. "You and your men don't need to apologize to us, Sir. The sons-of-bitches that did this to you won't ever do it to another American soldier. You're safe now and we're going to get all of you out of this camp back to the safety of our lines."

"How far away is the front, Sergeant?" asked Jack self-consciously.

"They're making good progress, but we're about forty miles behind enemy lines now. The line is being steadily pushed inland. We'll put out a defensive perimeter around the camp until we have the means to move all of you out. Beyond our Ranger outposts, Filipino guerrilla units have taken positions to block any Japanese attempt to reclaim the camp."

"Thank God you've come," cried the inmates in unison.

"We've been close by for the past twelve hours," informed the sergeant. "We laid low overnight in preparation for our attack on the compound at dawn. I see our Ranger Company Commander, Captain Horton heading our way. Captain Horton, this is Captain Ross and the men in his hut."

"It's an honor to meet you and your men, Captain Ross. Your courage and perseverance has been an inspiration to all of us. I'm sorry that we did not come sooner. We've been planning this rescue mission for quite some time. Let me assure all of you that you were never forgotten. To the contrary, your safety and welfare has been a major concern in every move that was planned for the Luzon campaign. I'm going to ask you to be patient a little longer and we'll get you out of here and on your way back home." The tall sturdily built young Ranger captain surveyed the men around him with grim respect and concern. There was a calm, confident air about him that was encouraging. They were in capable hands!

"Captain Horton," announced a Ranger radio operator with a small compact high frequency unit on his back. "It's battalion headquarters, Sir."

"This is Horton. We've secured the compound but have not taken count yet." Captain Horton turned to Jack and asked, "Approximately how many Americans are in the camp, Captain Ross?"

"Our last tally was six hundred and forty men. We've been losing three or four men every day for weeks," replied Jack in a weak voice.

"My God," exclaimed Captain Horton. "Battalion! Listen carefully, I'm making a few changes to our plan. We've got to feed these men and supply them with at least rudimentary medications immediately or we're going to lose even more before we move out to the south. Do you understand me? I insist that you drop the following supplies for seven hundred men at this compound as soon as possible: (1) food rations, (2) a full field kitchen capable of handling seven hundred men, (3) fatigue uniforms, including socks and footwear, (4) assorted preventative medicines for tropical duty, especially a large supply of antibiotics and quinine, and (5) a few more paramedics would be helpful. We have a severe medical emergency on our hands. Minutes are lives. In the name of God, don't fail us, and hurry! Out."

The stunned inmates heard the conversation and were impressed with the urgency in which he demanded food and medicine. Some of the men were still disbelieving that their deliverance was being accomplished. They habitually looked around for the omnipresent Japanese guards. All they saw were dead bodies and well-armed Rangers that had risked their lives to set them free before the fanatical guards could massacre them as they had planned to do.

Captain Horton inspected the Japanese warehouse and barracks complex, hoping to find facilities that the inmates could use to bathe or shower. None were available. The Japanese had used a mountain stream that ran close to their barracks for washing clothes and bathing. He judged that the highest priority for the men was nourishing food that they could digest. The Japanese facilities would be adequate for emergency use until their own field kitchens arrived. He had his men prepare a hot meal of rice soup, which had been the inmates main stay. The Japanese stocks contained canned chicken and a large supply of rice and canned vegetables. A high nutrition meal of vegetables, chicken and rice was prepared to increase protein intake. It was a meal most of the inmates could readily digest. Rich foods with fats would have been disastrous on their shrunken stomachs. Most would not have been able to keep it down no matter how badly they craved it.

Feeding the men all they could eat of the same type of food they were accustomed to eating seemed the best way of quickly increasing needed nourishment. They ate large quantities of rice. Some inmates returned to the steaming pots three or four times for more rice. It was the first time in three years that they had a chance to eat enough at one sitting to satisfy their hunger. Full stomachs made a difference. If there were any doubts in some of their minds about going home, they were dispelled. Good-natured bantering took place as the men felt the renewing power of adequate food. The reality that they had survived an epic ordeal was an empowering emotion that left most of them speechless.

The Rangers looked after the men with tenderness and respect, character traits that are a traditional mark of the American soldier. The ex-prisoners were the same brave men who had held off the Japanese at Bataan for a long time until their food, medicine, and ammunition ran out. They never ran out of guts. The Battling Bastards of Bataan had already secured their place in the history books, and the Rangers looked up to the proud inmates as heroes. Very quickly they walked a little taller, and were soldiers once again.

The Rangers set up a protective perimeter around the compound and that portion of the mountain stream where the men could bathe and clean themselves. Soap and towels were distributed with instructions to take as long as they wanted in the water. They planned to stay at the compound for the coming night. The inmates washed away layers of grime and filth allowing the healing power of water to renew their hopes and dreams. The brave Rangers watched the men frolic and play in the water like small children. The sight was worth any sacrifice they had made. Each Ranger wondered in their heart how well they would have done if placed in the same set of circumstances. The unspeakable cruelties the men had to endure would probably accompany them to their graves and the world would never know it had ever taken place, if for no other reason than it defied description.

Two hours after Captain Horton demanded help, four DC-3 transport planes circled the compound overhead and dropped parachutes loaded with supplies. Four P-51 Mustangs escorted the lumbering transports. One of the fighter planes buzzed the compound several times at a very low level to warn the men on the ground that chutes would be falling on them and they should be careful. Then the chutes began to float earthward. What a beautiful sight it was. It was a tangible manifestation that they were never forgotten and that they were still important to the nation. It was an image and an emotion they would never forget.

Shortly after the supply drop, those men who had already bathed in the stream were receiving their first rudimentary physical from the Ranger's medics and two additional paramedics that had jumped after the release of supplies. Routine statistics were recorded for each man. There were no records anywhere of the number of inmates in the compound, so a new roster was started. Men who normally weighed over one hundred pounds now weighed sixty to eighty pounds. Each inmate was treated for worms, malaria and dysentery. External wounds and abrasions were treated with the application of modern antibiotics, antiseptics and field dressings. Shoes, fresh underwear and socks were passed out as soon as the men bathed in the stream. New khaki shirts and pants were also distributed after their physical checkup. Now they looked and felt like soldiers! Pride was building by the hour.

More food was being processed on the portable field kitchens dropped by parachute. While the thorough physicals were being conducted, fresh bread was being baked. The aroma filled the camp evoking memories of better days. The bakers started handing out hot bread as soon as it came from the ovens.

The men gave the industrious bakers a rousing three cheers. Life was beginning to be good...

That night, the Rangers manned defensive positions while the prisoners slept their last night at the compound. Jack smelled the freshness of his new khaki clothes. They were a little too long and large for him, but for the first time in many months he felt like a soldier again. His thoughts were filled with memories of the past three years and of the men who had died. Tears filled his eyes and sadness filled his heart when he remembered their comradeship and courage in the face of certain death in a land far from home and loved ones. He wasn't sure if he wept for them or for himself. He was going home. They had already preceded him to their eternal resting place where they would remain forever young, some mere boys of seventeen years. The fact that Jack had a chance to live and grow older was entertained with a slight tinge of guilt.

The next morning the inmates woke to the smell of fresh bread that again excited their appetites. The Ranger cooks had manned the kitchens all night producing a small mountain of bread loaves. Breakfast was composed of oatmeal with bread and cheese and bananas, the first fresh fruit they had eaten in three years. The meal was nourishing and rich in protein and not unduly demanding on their fragile digestive system, which was now being treated with modern medicine.

Captain Horton walked among the men while they were eating to make an announcement over the portable megaphone he carried. "I hope your night's rest was better than the previous one. The meal you're now eating will be the last one you'll have at the compound. We're going to move you a few miles to the south to a rail junction. It's the same one that brought you here in 1942. Those of you who cannot walk should tell your hut commander so that we can locate enough native Filipino carts pulled by water buffaloes to handle those who cannot walk the distance. Do not be proud. We're concerned for your health as much as for your safety.

"If enough carts cannot be located to transport every man, then we'll carry you on our backs if needed, and it'll be our privilege to deliver you to safety. Eat hearty, for the next meal may be delayed slightly."

As Captain Horton was speaking, small two-wheel carts drawn by massive water buffaloes began to appear out of the jungle, forming two parallel lines at the perimeter of the compound. The small framed Filipino owners walked beside the powerful beasts and patiently waited. They surveyed the compound staring in amazement at the fragile physical condition of the inmates. Jack had heard from the Rangers that these particular Filipinos were part of an extensive band of guerrilla fighters throughout the Philippine Islands. Several times they had planned to destroy the Japanese guard contingent and release the prisoners, but their band was not strong enough to accomplish the task. Now that the Rangers had eliminated the Japanese, the natives were anxious to contribute to the success of the mission.

The men in Jack's hut were assembled near the carts. Jack knew each man in his charge personally and selected those who would ride in the carts. About a third had to be assisted in some way. An hour after breakfast, the men had collected what personal belongings they possessed and were waiting to leave.

"Before we evacuate the compound," announced Captain Horton, "we're going to burn it. I'm sure that you men will want the privilege of seeing it go up in smoke. We're ready to roll, so let the torches be lit so that this place will never be used again."

Jack and a dozen men from his hut ran into the dark infested interior of the hut they had called home for three years of hell. They joyfully set it afire and watched it burn.

After the compound was nothing but a heap of smoldering ashes, they formed up with the slow moving buffalo carts and started their trek to the outside world and freedom. Emancipation from purgatory was underway!

Chapter Three

The slow moving file of men and buffalo-drawn wagons filled with the sick and injured followed a well-worn cart track through the jungle. Alert Ranger outpost sentries slowly shepherded the group southward. Several of the rescued men who believed they could make the trek on their own, began to stumble and lag behind. They were assisted by their comrades and protectors. Bamboo poles and blankets were used as litters for such an emergency. The carts were already filled to capacity. They were escaping from the isolation of the jungle to freedom and no one was to be left behind.

The twelve mile journey to the railhead was painful and exhausting. Army Air Corps planes escorted the column scouring either side of the trail for signs of the Japanese. Whenever they found recognizable signs of enemy concentrations, they obliterated it. The staccato of aerial gunfire ripped across the landscape with increased frequency the closer they got to the railhead. Airspace was the sole property of the United States Army Air Corps.

Filipino forces operating parallel to the cart track also ran into scattered remnants of Japanese troops. They eliminated them or called upon air support to help do the job. Captain Horton had ordered them to maintain a constant protective line around the column, impressing upon them that the integrity of the column was more important than destruction of enemy troops which could be bypassed and dealt with later.

The freedom-bound prisoners felt secure in the hands of their rescuers. The column moved steadily southward. The few nutritious meals the inmates had enjoyed before starting the march probably saved several of the more weakened individuals. Captain Ross and the Rangers periodically passed out several pieces of milk chocolate and Tootsie-Rolls along the way. It was good quick energy and savored by the half-starved men. Some men were unable to control their desires and gorged themselves with the rich chocolate. Captains Horton and Ross warned them to eat the candy slowly so that their bodies could get used to it over a period of time. Those who ignored the advice soon emptied their stomachs and had to be assisted for the rest of the way.

Rangers close to the column filled the inmates in on the progress of the war. General MacArthur's armies had landed at Lingayen Bay on Luzon and were rapidly expanding southward toward Clark Field and Manila. They were also heading towards the prison compound. The distance between the column and the front was shortening rapidly. The Allies were also closing in on Germany. The Rhine had already been crossed and Italy was about ready to surrender.

A railroad spur line ran from Lingayen Bay to the railhead the column was headed for. By the time the inmates arrived at the railhead the spur line would be secured by American troops. At that point, professional medical attention was available for them. Surgeons, doctors and nurses had set up a field dressing station and were prepared to handle any medical emergency.

Emaciated men, unrecognizable by their closest friends and relatives, patiently and persistently marched toward freedom. They left behind a world that they would never be able to describe to their loved ones. It was beyond the ability of most human beings to comprehend what they had endured for three years. The future was potentially anything they wanted it to be. Their ability to adapt to the present world by removing three years of death, destruction, and vile inhumanity against them, would determine the success or failure of their resolve to get on with life.

They were still apprehensive and lacked the energy to think about the distant future. The carts were filled with weary sick men with large heads and haunting eyes that stared with awe and wonder at the scenes around them, much like little children. They looked with unabashed worship to their rescuers for direction and answers. Fear of the unknown was a very real and widespread emotion. They were still fragile human beings, with some still teetering on the thin line between life and death.

Their primary defense against the bestiality of the Japanese and the reality of their containment was detachment and denial of what was taking place. Without that escape mechanism, more of the men would have gone mad and perished in the process. It had become such a conditioned reflex to their environment, that when the day of their release from the heavy hand of the Japanese came, they were slow to adapt to the new condition called freedom. Retreating to their individual private worlds allowed them to tolerate what was taking place around them. Most never shared that private sanctuary with others. Tears frequently filled the hollow empty eyes that looked but did not see. The Japanese had desperately tried to strip them of their pride and hope. To give in to the wishes of the enemy was a path to oblivion and most avoided it. The presence of the Rangers made it possible for them to abandon their life-sustaining emotional shutdown. Hope and thanksgiving was slowly displacing denial and indifference. It was not an easy adjustment to make. A few would never return from the fantasy world forced upon them. They followed their friends like sheep who had lost their way.

One aspect of starvation over a long period of time that the Rangers were completely unprepared to acknowledge was the crippling effect of blindness. Every inmate was afflicted to some degree with loss of sight. It varied in severity and had reached epidemic proportions by the time the Rangers overran the compound. Ten percent of the men were completely blind and were tenderly cared for by their friends and buddies. Some of the intrepid Rangers wiped tears from their eyes as they watched the pathetically helpless blind men make their way along the cart path with one hand on the shoulder of a friend or at the end of a short piece of rope tied between them. Sometimes those leading the blind were having trouble distinguishing who and what was near them. It was the blind leading the blind. It was a display of compassion and trust that fueled the resolve of the Rangers and cultivated a seething hatred for the Japanese.

Captain Jack Ross was still able to distinguish faces in the sunlight. It was more difficult when the sun began to settle and it got darker. It had been so long since he had seen a written page that he did not know if he would be able to read the words or not. He was leading Bob Turner, one of the blind men from his hut, with pieces of braided rags tied between them. Sergeant Bob Turner had been his company radio man on Bataan and had accompanied him into captivity. Jack felt responsible for Bob. They were both from Maine and had initially served in the Maine National Guard. Bob had served in the First World War. He was a small energetic man in his mid-forties. He had been a source of strength and experience in the art of soldiering. The younger men in the company called him "Pops." His easygoing disposition helped to sustain him through their years of imprisonment. He was loyal and devoted to Jack. They reminisced a lot about their home state of Maine. A strong bond of trust and respect had been built between them during their years of adversity.

"How are you doing, Bob?" asked Jack without looking back.

"I'm still following you, Captain," Bob replied in a low voice. "Is it true that the whole compound is underway?"

"Every one of us, Bob. The wagons are carrying those who can't walk. Ever since the Rangers started to feed us, we haven't lost a man. That's something to be thankful for. There's a sight off to my right that I'll always remember."

"What's that, Captain?" asked Bob.

"These Rangers are a special breed of soldiers. One of the inmates was having trouble keeping his place in the column. One of the Rangers, a husky corporal, slung his rifle over his shoulder and picked up the man and cradled him in his arms as if he was a child. The prisoner can't weigh more than ninety pounds," described Jack. "You may not realize it, Bob, but we're a part of history-in-the-making. We were never forgotten the way we originally imagined. This plan that has been executed by the Rangers is the result of some careful planning in the higher echelons of command."

"I suppose so," admitted Bob. "I hadn't thought of it that way. If you have any more of that chocolate, I could use another mouthful now."

Jack unwrapped a Tootsie-Roll and passed it to Bob just as small arms fire erupted on both sides of the column. It was instinctive to drop to the ground. Rapid bursts from sub-machine guns and M-1 rifles filled the air. A few seconds later two twin engine B-26 Marauders with cannon and machine guns concentrated in the nose of the fuselage made strafing passes to suppress enemy strongholds. The amount of ordnance delivered by the aircraft impressed the inmates. They started to cheer the awesome display of skill and power. It made them proud to be Americans.

Shortly the Rangers announced that all resistance had been eliminated and they could continue their march. The weary men returned to their place in the column. Uncertainty and despair was beginning to show up in the ranks. They were rapidly running out of strength to continue the march. Captain Horton took full measure of the abilities of the men and went on the radio to demand help, or a disaster may be in the making if he continued to push the former prisoners to the limit of their capacity. He contacted General Krueger's Sixth Army Field Headquarters at Lingayen Bay.

"This is Captain Horton," he announced in a firm voice. He knew that he was pushing beyond normal channels of command, but he needed more help than he was getting. He was talking with an old acquaintance. "I understand that all combat elements are fully extended, but I can't guarantee the welfare of the men we've collected from the prison compound. Listen carefully to me, Major. The men have reached the limit of their strength now. I repeat; they can't continue without assistance. I need help in the form of Jeeps, trucks, anything that can transport these American soldiers a few more miles to the railhead and safety. We'll provide security for them, but we cannot carry all of them on our backs without compromising that security. I need help and I need it now. These men deserve maximum effort."

"I understand your plight, Captain," replied the officer at the other end of the line. "I'll get something to you. How many men are we talking about?"

"I have approximately six hundred and fifty former prisoner about nine miles from the railhead. You better be sure that medical attention is available for them or we're going to lose some," warned Captain Horton.

"Word just came from General Krueger that you've got maximum effort, Captain. You and your company of Rangers have done a superb job. Well done."

"Thank you, Sir," the anxious Captain Horton signed off and ordered his men to halt the column so that they could take refuge in the shade of the trees off to the side of the roadway. "Find a convenient spot to relax. We'll distribute water and all of the cold rations we have with us. Help is on its way."

An hour later, an ad hoc column of Jeeps, two and a half ton trucks, LVT amphibious tractors and weapon carriers entered the shaded area. The vehicles were prepared to make shuttle runs to and from the railhead until all had been safely deposited at the rail junction. One hundred of the sick and invalid went on the first shuttle run. Four trips followed in a short sequence of time. Doctors and nurses were busy tending to the men at the railhead. Those who needed surgery or more demanding care were taken by ambulance to other nearby field dressing stations.

Jack was the last man to ride out of the jungle. A Dodge weapons carrier was waiting for him to climb aboard. He confronted Captain Horton and a number of his Rangers.

"On behalf of the rest of the compound I want to thank you and your men. You snatched us from certain death and we'll be forever grateful. What can a man say who has just been handed a reprieve from a miserable death? Thank you seems inadequate, but it's all that I can come up with right now...." Jack shook his hand and saluted him.

"Your safety has been a part of our daily lives for some time, Captain Ross. You've made us all proud. Every man in my

29

company has been trained to do what we did here on Luzon. After we secured the prison compound, every one of us asked ourselves if we had the courage and stamina to absorb the punishment and humiliation you and your men have endured for more than three years. Yours is a special kind of moral courage and strength that few people are ever asked to draw from. We who have never had to face that level of testing stand in awe of the spirit that sustained you. The best of luck, Captain Ross. May our good Lord continue to look down on you with favor."

"Thank you..."

Things happened quickly once the men were transported to the railhead in the vehicles. The large medical detachment acted as a clearing house for the patients and dispersed them to various other field hospitals. By the time the third shuttle arrived with their riders the previous two had already been dispatched to waiting facilities.

The railroad did not have a locomotive to pull the cars over the rails, so the Army modified several GMC 2 1/2 Ton Army Trucks with three drive axles fitted with steel flanged wheels that rolled between the rails. They were noisy but it was an efficient piece of resourcefulness that did the job.

Jack helped organize the men as they filed through the medical tent set up beside the rails. He took his place as the last man from the prison compound before he was processed and checked over thoroughly. It was no surprise that he was suffering from malaria and several other tropical diseases, some unknown to the medical teams, yet, he was able to move relatively freely about without discomfort. He received a series of antibiotic injections and a massive dose of quinine to ease his symptoms of malaria. The thing that frightened Jack the most was his partial blindness and the nagging fear that it was going to be permanent. The doctors tried to encourage him that he would regain normal vision as soon as his body chemistry was placed in balance. He needed to eat well and regain some of the weight he had lost. They informed him that he would be placed on a Navy hospital ship now located at Lingayen Gulf.

An Army field kitchen was set up beside the medical tent. When Jack finished the physical checkup, he walked to the mess tent and took his place at the end of the chow line. He was interrupted by a young corporal who insisted that he take his place at the front of the line. Jack thanked him and received three rousing cheers from the young soldiers. He felt good being with his own kind after a long absence.

Jack filled his tray with pork and gravy over mashed potato, green beans and a bowl of fruit cocktail. How often he had dreamed of food like this. Taking a bench seat at a table in the mess tent he ate slowly, savoring every mouthful. A mess sergeant came to his table with a pitcher of cold milk and a chilled glass.

"I still can't believe that this is happening to me," exclaimed Jack, overwhelmed with emotion. He wiped tears from his eyes with pencil thin fingers clenched in a fist not much larger than that of a small child.

"Welcome back, Sir," said the mess sergeant, pouring a glass of milk for him. "I personally purchased this fresh milk from a nearby farm. We especially wanted to have it for you and your men. Eat heartily, Sir."

"Thank you, Sergeant. Milk has been a part of my fantasies for three years. I appreciate your thoughtfulness."

"You're very welcome, Sir."

Jack drank three glasses of milk and finished his meal with a helping of coffee ice cream, compliments of the U.S. Navy. Other former prisoners were coming through the chow line. Several officers sat at the table with Jack. He had been acting as senior officer of the camp for the past few months since the withdrawal of a colonel into a world of his own. Many of the officers, like the enlisted men, were being distributed to various medical facilities, some Army and some Navy. The officers of the compound had made a pact amongst themselves that once the war was over, the surviving officers had an obligation to contact the families of the men who died in prison. The intent was to inform the survivors how their loved ones lived and died. An accurate record was kept of every deceased soldier's name and home address.

31

Jack committed himself to contact those who had lived within New England. There were seven in all, three from Maine, one from New Hampshire, one from Vermont and two from Massachusetts. Jack said good-bye to his fellow officers and men. It was an emotionally powerful moment for them. He was surprised how difficult it was to go their separate ways after sharing years of privation and the horrors of internment together. Reluctantly, he boarded the Army truck- powered train heading for Lingayen Gulf. One hundred of his men accompanied him.

Chapter Four

Captain Jack Ross awoke from a malaria induced black-out to the sound of a woman's voice. He was wet with sweat. His malaria had kicked up on the train, and the last thing he remembered was falling over in the seat watching the walls and ceiling go around and around. He felt hot and cold at the same time and was shivering from head to toe.

"Where am I?" he cried out hysterically. He stared at the ceiling, the cleanest thing he had seen in years. No one answered him so he called out again, "Where am I?"

"I'm sorry to make you wait," answered a nurse with a soft melodious voice. He had been hearing that voice and he was afraid that he had died. She sounded like an angel! "You're on a Navy Hospital ship and we're going to take good care of you, Captain Ross." She reached for his arm to take his pulse. "What can I do for you?" She wore a Naval Nurse headband with an ensign rate and filled the ship's ward with a serene calmness felt by everybody in her care.

"I don't remember anything. I was on the train when I passed out. May I have a drink of water? My mouth feels hot and dry," Jack requested in a low voice. "I thought I was going to an Army hospital."

"I'll get you some water. You should drink all you can. My name is Ensign Kelly. The Navy is fighting the war too, Captain. We have about thirty soldiers in the ward with you, some from the same prison camp you were in." She held a straw in a cold glass of water to his parched lips. It was cool and felt good on his dry throat.

"Thank you, Ensign. That was refreshing. I feel weaker now than when we walked out of the prison compound."

33

"That's because of the fever from the malaria virus. It's going to take some time. Your resistance to disease has been drastically altered by malnutrition. We're going to change that. Let us care for you and do our job, Captain. You just concentrate on getting well."

"I will, Ensign. I'm lucky to be alive... Many didn't make it...," Jack replied with slurred words. The sedative she had given him in the glass of water was starting to work. "Rest easy, Captain," she said, wondering what horror stories his head was filled with. She checked the glucose solution tube in his arm and took his pulse again. It was racing wildly. Even in sleep he was nervously agitated.

Later, Jack witnessed an event that he would never forget. His bed was positioned so that he had a clear, unobstructed view of the bed of a patient being treated by Ensign Kelly. She bent over the wounded soldier to whisper something in his ear. Jack saw a sad, forlorn look on her face. Her voice was soothing and comforting. She administered medicine into the soldier's arms and reassured him that she was with him. The angel of mercy remained there until there was no more life in the shattered inert body. She tenderly closed the wide-open eyelids and pulled a white sheet over the soldier's head. Ensign Kelly stood over the body for a long time, weeping in silence. The scene was etched in Jack's soul.

That evening, after the ship's ward was settled for the night and lights were dimmed, Jack was experiencing a strange phenomenon. He couldn't sleep on the soft bed. Years of sleeping on the solid ground had become a habit, so he threw a blanket on the deck and slept soundly. The next morning the duty nurse was alarmed at what he had done. In the process of getting out of bed to sleep on the floor, he had pulled the glucose line from his arm and it leaked all over the deck.

"Captain Ross," the nurse exclaimed. "What in the world has happened to you? You've pulled the sugar and water line from your arm. Did you fall out of bed?"

"No," he replied shyly. "The bed was too soft, so I decided to sleep on the floor. I've been sleeping on the hard ground for three years."

"Too soft?" she asked incredulously, then smiled at his discomfort. "Would you please climb back on this bed so that I can reconnect your glucose line? You need the solution more than anyone else. You've been dehydrated to a serious level."

"I'm sorry nurse. I apologize for making a mess. I wasn't thinking."

"Never mind, Captain. Accidents happen to all of us. I want to take your vitals again before breakfast. Are you hungry?"

"Oh, yes. It seems that the more I eat, the more I'm hungry. Food tastes so good. I used to gripe about Army chow like everybody else. From now on, I vow to be appreciative of any food I receive."

"The barber will be in to see you after breakfast. He'll give you a shave and a haircut. Then we'll give you a shaving kit so that you can take care of yourself."

"I'll look forward to that, nurse. Thanks for everything," Jack said.

Shortly, Jack sat in a straight-backed chair for the pharmacist mate to cut his hair. It was similar to a boot camp crew cut. The young pharmacist said that the hair was a ready host of several types of insects and infectious causal agents. The main reason for the crew cut was not for appearance, but for personal hygiene. A foamy shampoo followed the haircut. Now he was thoroughly sanitized, and he instantly felt better and looked healthier.

Jack was resting on his hospital bed when Ensign Kelly entered the ward with an Army officer. "Captain Ross, you have a visitor, Captain Swenson." She cranked up his bed and left.

"How are you feeling, Captain Ross?" asked Captain Swenson.

"Compared to the last three years, I feel that I've just been placed in the lap of luxury. I'm feeling fine, a little weak and a little rough around the edges, but I'm improving hourly."

"So I understand. May I call you Jack? My friends call me Swede," announced the tall raw-boned Army captain.

"Please do, Swede," answered Jack.

"I'm an intelligence officer with the Sixth Army and I wanted to discuss a few things with you. I understand that you've already been debriefed."

"Yes, on the rail car on our way to Lingayen Gulf."

"When was the last time you had word from home, Jack?"

"It was in 1942. I have the last letter I received from my wife Myla just prior to our surrender on Bataan."

"Where did you lose your dog tags?"

"A few days before the surrender, I was hit by a mortar round or an artillery shell and was wounded on my back. I lost my dog tags and helmet in the same explosion. It was near the coast because I recall being able to see Corregidor while I was lying in the mud."

"I hate to be the one to tell you, Jack, but your tags were found by a Catholic Chaplain who made his way to Australia. He turned your tags over to the Far East Command, which was General MacArthur. Your next of kin were notified that you were missing in action and presumed to be dead. A thorough check of the International Red Cross records of prisoners of the Japanese camps failed to come up with your name. We also scoured the muster lists of guerrilla groups throughout the Philippines and came up empty."

"As far as I know we never received one piece of mail. We never received Red Cross packages either and we were not allowed to send out letters from our compound," Jack added, concerned about the implications of the conversation.

"Without any evidence of your being in captivity or with partisan groups, the Army changed your status to deceased instead of missing."

"My God, my wife, Myla thinks I'm dead?"

"I'm afraid so, Jack. It's an ugly foul up, but under the circumstances known to everybody at that time and place, it was a logical conclusion. The Army will be contacting your wife and father to set the record straight."

"When this hospital ship arrives at Pearl Harbor will I be able to call home from there?" Jack asked.

"Of course, you should do that just as soon as possible. I apologize for the sorrow this error has caused your wife and father. I'm sorry this had to happen."

"I suppose this situation is favorable to the reverse – failure to notify a family that their loved one has been killed in action."

"There's another item I wanted to discuss with you," explained Swede.

"My time is your time. I'm not going anywhere."

"I've talked to several of the prisoners that were with you at the camp. They told me that you would be talking with seven of the deceased men's families in the New England area. Is that correct?"

"Yes, the officers of the camp all agreed that we owed that to the memory of a lot of brave men. Our promise to sit with the families and share with them how their loved one died is a commitment all of us will be proud to honor. Are there any problems with that?"

"No, I applaud the commitment to your men. I simply wanted to pass on to you that every prisoner alive or dead is eligible for the Combat Infantryman's Badge. The Army will supply you with these badges when you get well. I have one with me for you, Jack."

"Thanks, Swede. It's the most sought after award in the Army. I'll be proud to wear it. I'm glad we had this conversation. I'll make it a point to call home as soon as I can. My poor Myla must be having a difficult time."

"I wish you lots of luck, Jack. Good-bye."

"So long, Swede."

Ensign Kelly stopped by his bed to take his temperature and blood pressure. She had an easy touch and took an interest in each of her patients.

"How do you feel, Captain?"

"I'm doing better than I expected, Ensign. I've gained about six pounds since I left the compound. I didn't say much to the doctor when he made his rounds; maybe you can help me," he suggested hesitantly.

"I'll do what I can," she answered in her distinctive soft voice.

"I started to lose some of my vision a year or so ago. I can't even read a newspaper! Is there anything you might suggest? Is it really true that sight loss caused by starvation will return once a nutritional balance has been accomplished?" His voice reflected the deep concern and panic that accompanied the knowledge of being permanently blind. "I have trouble distinguishing facial features. I'm quite sure that you're a blonde, but I cannot see your eyes even when you're close to my bed."

"Yes, I'm a blonde, Captain. I've heard the doctors discuss the high percentage of blindness with you former prisoners. The consensus of opinion is that sight will eventually be restored. That should encourage you, Captain. I'll speak to the doctor about glasses for you. I know that the ship does not have lens grinding facilities aboard. They're available at Pearl. I'll let you know."

"Thanks, Ensign."

The next day when Ensign Kelly came on duty, she had a pair of glasses and a bundle of newspapers and magazines in her hand for Jack.

"I have something that will help you, Captain Ross. The ship has a supply of these magnifying glasses. Try a set on," she said, wiping the lens and placing them on him.

"Wow, what a difference they make. Things far away are still blurred, but I can see print, and now I can see you, Ensign. When I came on board the ship and first heard your voice I thought it was the voice of an angel. You're beautiful, Ensign, just like I imagined you to be," confessed Jack, blushing heavily.

She noted the blush and smiled. "Thank you, Captain. I'll bet you say that to every girl."

"No," answered Jack seriously. "The only other girl I've said that to is my wife, Myla. She's a teacher."

"She's a lucky woman to have a husband like you. The war is over for you, Captain. She'll be happy to have you come home."

"I'm sure," he answered, closing his eyes. "An Army intelligence officer just told me that I've been listed as killed in action since 1942. She'll be surprised to hear from me when we reach Pearl Harbor."

"That will be a day of thanksgiving for your family," said Ensign Kelly, placing the magazines and papers on the stand beside the bed. "You'll be able to browse through this reading material at your leisure, Captain."

"Thanks, Ensign Kelly. I appreciate your thoughtfulness."

"Incidentally, you're scheduled for a visit to the dentist first thing in the morning."

"That's fine. I'm impressed with the quality of care the Navy dispenses. On behalf of my men I want to thank all of you for your generous professionalism and sensitivity. The men have been through a lot. I could not ask for better care than you're giving them. Your family must be very proud of you."

Ensign Kelly heard the words and knew they were sincere and heartfelt. "You're generous with your compliments, Captain, but thank you just the same. You and your men deserve the best."

The next morning, Jack learned that the teeth he had lost could be replaced with a dental plate made up by the specialist on board the ship. By the time he reached Pearl Harbor he would be wearing the plate.

Two months later, Jack's hair had grown enough so that he requested a light trim by the ship's barber before leaving the ship. The night before he was scheduled to leave the ship for the Naval Hospital at Pearl Harbor, he came down with a high fever. Malaria had struck again. He thrashed around in a feverish state. The doctors gave him a mild sedative and a concentrated dose of quinine. He was unaware of being moved from the ship. His spasmodic restlessness was eased by the sedative.

The staff at the large Naval Hospital on the shore of Pearl Harbor close to the sunken hulk of the USS Arizona told Captain Ross that he was going to need a long convalescing period to insure a complete recovery. His health was fragile. His weight loss had dropped to a dangerous level. The doctors concluded that part of what was allowing him to function at all was his iron will and concern for the welfare of his men. He would stay at the hospital until his recovery and weight gain were normal and complete.

For three days he sweat and tossed in his new bed at the hospital. The staff worked tirelessly to lower his temperature to acceptable limits. They resorted to immersions in cold water and monitored his heart continuously. It was harsh treatment, but the doctors were afraid that the high temperatures could trigger a decline into a coma, and his fragile ability to resist was questionable. Jack protested the extremes of hot and cold. One minute he felt that he was burning up, and the next minute he started shivering from cold chills. There was no happy medium. He was exhausted and just wanted to go to sleep. The staff was concerned for his chances to survive without some brain damage from the high temperature spikes he experienced.

On the fourth day, Jack's temperature began to recede and he was able to take some liquid and eat some oatmeal. Myla was constantly on his mind. He desperately wanted to call home to hear her voice again, and was finally given permission to make the call to the mainland after eating lunch. There was a difference of five hours between Wells, Maine, and Hawaii. The staff warned him that all calls were monitored, and if he started to divulge names of military units or any information the censors think could be of help to the enemy, his line would be cut immediately.

Jack first placed a call to their cottage at Kennebunkport. It took a while for the lines to clear. Finally it rang once and an operator with a Maine accent came on the line to announce that the number he had called was no longer in service at that time. He was afraid that something had happened and called his father's number.

The phone rang once and Jack heard the familiar voice of his father. "Hello."

"Hello, Dad. Don't be alarmed to hear my voice. Can you hear me okay?"

"Yes, I hear you, Jack. I can't believe it's you, Son. When the word came from the government that you were dead, I didn't want to believe it. I prayed for you every day, Son, and now my prayers have been answered. I received a call from the

Army last month. They said that there had been a mistake. They told me that you're alive, so I've been expecting your call. What a relief to hear your voice. You sound weak and tired. Where are you?"

"I'm at Pearl Harbor, Dad. I was in a prison camp for over three years. I'll tell you more about it when I come home. I'm at a Naval Hospital. They're taking good care of me, so don't worry about me anymore, Dad. I tried to call Myla at the cottage and the operator told me that the line had been disconnected. Where is she?" Jack anxiously asked to speak to his wife.

"Son, I have news for you that will be difficult for you to understand. If you're not sitting you should brace yourself..."

"Has something happened to her?" he cried with alarm.

"No, she's all right. I see her several times a week. The Army has also contacted her about you. When they delivered your dog tags to her with the warning that you were missing and presumed dead, it was a terrible time for us, Son."

"I can understand that, Dad. What are you trying to tell me?" Jack was irritated at his father's reluctance to tell him what he wanted to know.

"A few months after that first notice, the Army informed her that you were dead. That was about May of 1942. I don't know how to tell you except straight out. Myla married Jeff Snow a few months ago...."

Chapter Five

"What do you mean, she's married to Jeff Snow? She's my wife!" Jack snapped angrily.

"I'll try to explain it the best I can, Son. I know how hard this news must be on you. It's difficult to know what to say," his father patiently explained. "When can you come home?"

"Not for a while, Dad. You wouldn't recognize me the way I look now."

"If I had a magic wand to make everything the way it was, I'd wave it now, but I don't, Son. My heart aches for you, and I can't ease your pain. I know how much you two meant to each other. Seeing the two of you together always made me feel good for both of you."

"Sure, we meant a lot to each other," repeated Jack sarcastically in a high pitched tone. He could not believe what his father was telling him. "You don't seem to be very upset about it, Dad!"

"Listen, Son. No matter what you think or how angry you are, the fact remains that it has taken place. I'm not asking you to accept the fact without some agonizing reaction; that's only natural. Try to understand what Myla went through. Since the war started I've been closer to her than ever before. Her love and loyalty never faltered, Jack, never. You must believe that because it's a fact that cannot be denied. For three years she waited, believing that you were dead. I know it hurts, Son, but try not to take all of your anger out on Myla. I don't know what else to say about it except that it's a horrible catastrophe for the two of you, and you can blame the war."

Jack had no intention of placing blame on his father. It was not fair to use him as a sounding board for his frustrations and anger. He deserved better than that from his only son who loved him.

"I'm sorry, Dad. I didn't mean to strike out at you. I'll be here at Pearl Harbor for a while longer."

"How serious is your condition, Son?" His father was concerned. Jack had not talked about his health problems.

"I've got malaria and I'm undernourished as a result of my prison confinement, but I'm making progress. I've got to hang up, Dad. There's a long line of sailors who want to use the phones. I love you. We'll have a chance to talk more when I come home."

"Good luck, Son. I'm sorry that this call has to be so painful for you. As for me, I feel like rejoicing. My son is alive and soon I'll be able to give him a bear hug. I'm thankful for that. Take care of yourself and get well soon."

"I will, Dad, and you do the same."

Jack returned to his ward and climbed on the bed, numbed with disbelief. His wife was married to another man! How could such a thing be? He stared at the ceiling for the rest of the night feeling empty, lifeless, and very much betrayed. He hurt too much to cry; it was just so inexplicable. The more he thought about the situation, the more infuriated he became. The feeling of impotence was the hardest to deal with. His anger and disgust were more intense than the hurt. A husband had a right to expect more from his wife. Myla became the object of his animosity.

Recovery for Jack was months down the road. He knew that he had to do something to get Myla out of his mind until he had a chance to confront her face to face and demand an explanation. He began his long recovery with a renewed focus and commitment to first things first. He had to regain his health before anything else in his life could be addressed. One evening after he had called his father, Jack was sitting in the solarium overlooking the harbor with a hospital bathrobe over him. Staring at the blackened hulks of twisted metal, he tried to imagine the terror that had taken place aboard those ships that settled to the bottom encasing hundreds of men in their fiery tombs. He was fortunate compared to the fate of the young sailors that still remained inside the rusty black superstructures.

A soft breeze blew across the water, filling the solarium with the exotic aromas of tropical plants and flowers. He was still angry at Myla, but his distress was lessened when he thought of the blazing inferno the sailors had to face with no hope of escape. Their fate saddened him. At least he would be able to go home and live a normal life, even if it was without Myla. All was not lost, he rationalized. Suddenly, without warning, thoughts of Myla filled his heart with memories he had treasured over the years, and they plunged him to the depths of despair. Tears started to flow. There were so many things he had wanted to share with her. His love for her had sustained him for three years when all else had failed. He had relived every second of their last days together at the cottage on the ocean over and over again. Now… it was all for nothing; she had failed him, too.

An avalanche of emotion flooded through him. Ever since the conversation with his father, Jack had forced himself to not think about Myla. The denial demanded all of his discipline and strength, for she had been a large part of his life for many years. Sweat beads formed on his brow. His body was wracked with convulsive sobs. He had so much wanted to hear her voice and hear her say that she loved him. He needed that as much as he needed life itself. Without Myla there was no life. He felt more alone sitting on the solarium at Pearl Harbor than he did at the prison compound. Myla had robbed him of hope and dashed the dreams he had fashioned for their future.

"Are you all right, Captain Ross?" asked a soft voice. Jack was too wrapped up in his grief to hear anything. Ensign Lorena Kelly placed a reassuring hand on his shoulder and asked again: "Are you all right, Captain?"

"I'm okay," answered Jack. "Is that you, Ensign Kelly?"

"Yes," she said in her easy reassuring voice. "I saw you out here and was worried that something had gone wrong. Can I help with anything?"

"No," he answered, turning away, embarrassed that she had seen him like this. "I thought you were still on the hospital ship."

"I requested shore duty. I had three years on the ship and thought it was time to change." She saw his embarrassment and correctly read his desire to be alone. "I'm sorry to have intruded. If you need anything, just call."

"What I need you can't provide, Ensign, but I appreciate your asking," explained Jack in a wavering voice.

He remained in the solarium for another two hours until Ensign Kelly came to request that he return to his bed. She needed to hook him up to his glucose solution for intravenous feeding. He obeyed her request and quickly climbed into the bed, closing his swollen red eyes. She noted his withdrawn condition. He was holding a lot of pain inside.

"Captain Ross, I don't want to interfere with your affairs, but sometimes it helps to talk things over. We have several Navy Chaplains on board who would be pleased to talk with you if you want. It's just a suggestion. You can let me know."

"Maybe you've touched on something that would help. I'd be glad to have one stop by. I'm not a regular church-going-man, but I do believe in the Almighty. Thanks for recommending it."

"You're welcome, soldier," she said, hanging a glucose bottle on a post at the head of the bed.

"Do you mind if I ask you a question, Ensign?"

"I never know how to answer a question like that, Captain, but if I can help I'll do my best," she answered haltingly.

"If you were happily married and were notified that your husband was killed in action, would you marry another man after two and a half years?" he asked in a shaky voice.

The question was very personal. Her husband had been a pilot and was killed in a bombing mission over Germany in 1943. She had successfully suppressed the pain his loss had created so that she could do her job as he would have wanted her to do. Hearing Captain Ross ask such a question brought back some of the memories. She searched for an answer to the question. Evidently it was the root cause of his distress. His wife must have married another man and now her husband is alive and will soon be coming home. What a horrible prescription for a heartache, she thought before answering.

"I can't answer that with assurance or authority, Captain. It would depend on a lot of things which I cannot predict. Let me say that if the lady was certain that her husband was dead, then she waited a reasonable period of time to grieve his loss. Every person handles tragedy in a different way. I don't want to judge her, but if you're looking for something or someone to blame, place it on the war. It has brought heartache to thousands of people and families. You know that more than most people. It's easy to fall into self-pity if we're not careful. I speak from experience on that. It can consume you if it's not held in check. I'm not sure if my answer has helped or not. Now, I do have to continue my rounds. I've given you a small sedative on doctor's orders. Goodnight, Captain."

"Goodnight, Ensign. You're right; the war has changed a lot of things...."

Over the next two months Jack experienced a dramatic convalescent period at the hospital. He was gaining a pound a day in weight and grew steadily stronger. The doctors told him that his malaria was under control unless he went back to the tropics and became infected again. His vision was slowly being restored to near normal except for his ability to distinguish fine print. They made up a pair of prescription glasses for his use when reading. After he had attained most of his normal weight, the hospital discharged him to the Naval Physical Therapy Center nearby on the harbor water front. The weight he had gained had to be molded and conditioned to the same point he had been before his incarceration.

"Well, Captain Ross," announced Ensign Kelly, watching him pack his duffel bag for the transfer to the therapy center barracks. "You've improved greatly from the person we picked up at Lingayen Gulf. Congratulations. I wish you luck at the therapy center. You won't find it easy over there."

"So I've heard, Ensign," replied Jack, checking his necktie in a mirror. "I leave here a better man than when you picked me up in the Philippines. Much of my progress I owe to you and the doctors here. I'll never forget the transition I had to make from prison to freedom to the luxury of being cared for by competent caregivers. Thank you for all the special treatment."

"It has been a pleasure, Captain."

"May I ask you for a favor?"

"I still don't know how to answer that question," she laughed and he joined in, extending his hand to her.

"I've been promoted to major. These are my new bronze oak leaves. Would you please fasten them to my shoulder strap?"

"It'll be a privilege, Major," she said, accepting the two leaves. "You deserve the rank and the Combat Infantryman's Badge you're wearing. I'm familiar with the desirability of the badge to you Army men. You join a select group. Congratulations."

"Thanks, Ensign, I'm glad to be out of the hospital; however, I'll miss the pleasant atmosphere that always reigned supreme in your wards. It has been swell being under your care. Good-bye, Ensign Kelly."

"Good-bye, Major Ross," she saluted. "Take care of yourself."

Jack left the hospital pleased that he had done so well. He turned at the elevator door for one last look at Ensign Kelly and saw her waving to him. Suddenly he was reluctant to leave. He was probably in love with the attractive nurse, just like every other wounded serviceman in her care. He returned the wave and stepped into the elevator.

The Physical Therapy Center was the final destination for wounded or sick men before being reassigned to units or on their way to civilian life. He enrolled at the center and was assigned a room at the barracks and to a class of twenty soldiers. Three of them were from the prison compound with Jack. They assembled for an orientation session where he spotted Bob Turner wearing glasses. They hardly recognized the way each other looked in their uniforms.

"So you wear the bronze leaves now. Congratulations, Sir, you deserve it. You look like a new man," greeted Bob.

"Hi, Bob. It's nice to see a familiar face. How are you doing with the glasses?"

"My sight has not completely returned. The glasses make up for the difference. I was scared that it would be permanent."

"We've come a long way, Bob. It won't be long before we leave the therapy center and head home to Maine. I can hardly wait."

"Me, too."

"Gentlemen," announced a well-built pharmacist chief with a large number of hash marks on his left sleeve indicating years of service. "I'm Chief Conray. Welcome to our Physical Therapy Center. You'll be going through a demanding series of exercises that will make new people out of you. At times you'll hurt and be uncomfortable, but believe me, the end result will please you. You're going to work together as a class unit. That means we help each other. The therapist in charge is Lieutenant Patti Tenaki."

The name Tenaki hit most of the men where it hurt the most. Hatred of anything Japanese had been so deeply ingrained that it was a natural response. Chief Conray held his arms out to a short Hawaiian nurse with long black hair down to her shoulders. She wore lieutenant bars. The disbelief, outrage and dark disappointment for some of the men was so strong it could be felt throughout the room. An ominous silence settled over the group. Someone called her a god-damned-Jap loud enough that she heard the epitaph. She ignored the rejection and smiled at the audience.

"I'm Lieutenant Patti Tenaki. I'm a registered nurse and a certified physical therapist. I want to help you mend the scars left by the war." She paused for a long time and slowly scanned the room making eye contact with each person. She never blinked an eyelid. Her petite build was enhanced by the white Naval Nurse uniform she wore with pride. She moved about at the front of the room with grace and dignity in the face of almost unanimous rejection and much hatred on the part of her audience. Jack thought it was in bad taste.

"I'm not a Jap," she explained calmly. "I'm a native Hawaiian citizen with Japanese parents. I graduated from

Honolulu High School and have a degree in nursing from Boston University. Those men who object to me as their therapist may leave the room now and join another class assembling two doors down the corridor on the left. You may join that group with no questions asked." She continued to scan the faces of the group. Three men left, raising their voices in crude language about her ancestry. She watched them leave with a proud tilt of her head.

"Those who left the room have my sympathy and my forgiveness. I understand your distrust, hatred, and anger. If I were in your shoes I would probably feel the same way. So maybe, with your group, we have a chance to rebuild your bodies and shape your anger so that you can direct it towards those who deserve it. Sure, I look like a Japanese enemy because it is my ancestry, and I dearly love my parents. If you knew them you would like them, too.

"I have two brothers who joined the U. S. Army. They fought in Sicily and Italy. One was killed in action at Anzio. The other is fighting somewhere in France as we speak. He has proven his devotion to this country we all serve with pride. He wears the Medal of Honor, this country's highest award for valor above and beyond. So it's all right if you hate those who've brutalized you and your buddies. Just don't let that blind hatred rule your thoughts for others that have not harmed you. It's all right for you to dislike me for the way I do things or if I make mistakes or unintentionally hurt you; but please, don't dislike me for my ancestry. You men have my respect, my admiration, and my sympathy for the horrors you've had to endure. I join you in denouncing the inhuman treatment those of you who were prisoners of war in the Japanese camps had to endure. I hope that over the period of our course I can earn your respect. All I ask of you is the opportunity to serve you. When we've finished the course, I'm confident you'll thank me and feel better about yourself."

The room was silent. She looked apprehensively from one side of the room to the other hoping to see acceptance of her offer. Jack saw an intelligent and compassionate young lady with a lot of grit asking for permission to help them heal their bodies. He was thankful to be alive and was glad to applaud her for taking such a courageous stand. He raised his arms above his head and began clapping his hands. One by one the other men in the group followed his example. Lieutenant Tenaki was afraid that she had drawn a negative response and was nervously fingering the file folders she held in her hands. Then she saw Jack raise his arms. She smiled and held her hand across her mouth like a little girl. Her eyes watered. She wiped away the tears with a handkerchief as the hall erupted in unanimous applause.

"Thank you, thank you," she cried. "The routines we're going to follow will be demanding but we'll do it as a team. We're going to take your bodies and mold them back to their original condition. Our aim is to fine-tune them into the precision instruments they were intended to be. At the end you'll be able to go out there and take on the world on your terms. One more thing before we start, I'd like the privilege of calling each of you by your first names. This is no place for titles. I have the roster list here and will familiarize myself with your names as we go along. Most who know me call me Miss Patti. You can call me other things but not to my face," she laughed energetically.

Jack had a feeling that this was going to be a fun session. Miss Patti was going to keep their butts humping more than a tough drill sergeant, and she was going to do it with a smile and a laugh as she pushed them to their limits. He was prepared to run the gauntlet.

Chapter Six

Jack had gained eighty percent of his weight back and was pleased with the achievement. He thought he was in reasonably good condition before starting the routines at the therapy center; however, the first day under Miss Patti's tutelage dispelled that myth. Strenuous stretching, walking, and jumping exercises completely exhausted him at the end of the first day. Miss Patti was a bundle of energy and stamina. She worked tirelessly with the men encouraging them when they lagged behind or slacked off in effort. She was a demanding taskmaster who continued to push and pull them to their limits. "If you don't hurt at the end of the routines, you haven't been trying hard enough," was a statement often heard by the group.

The men soon forgot that she was of Japanese ancestry. She was an attractive woman with impish ways. When she was dressed in her Naval Nurse uniform, some considered her beautiful. Jack looked upon her as cute and in many of her mannerisms and actions she reminded him of Myla except that Myla was much more reserved.

Jack used his time at the center to bring some order to his life. Myla remained a large part of everything he thought about. She was still his wife, and he simply did not know what to do about the situation. Myla never contacted him. He knew that nothing could be accomplished until he had a face to face discussion with her. In the meantime he worked hard to get from one day to another. The war could not last more than another year. He had not made up his mind about continuing a military career. Much depended on Myla. He was lucky he had a choice of two careers that he was comfortable with. Many men didn't know what they wanted out of life. He was strong enough to survey his options and to postpone any decisions until he talked to Myla.

On May 8, 1945 the radios announced that Germany had surrendered. Victory in Europe, V-E Day, was rejoiced all over the world. One enemy down, one more to go! The large therapy room erupted in cheers and whistles. Miss Patti had announced it to them early in the afternoon. "We've just received an official communiqué from the Department of the Navy that Germany has surrendered unconditionally. The war in Europe is over." She clapped her hands and embraced those around her. "We'll celebrate by playing hooky. We'll pick it up tomorrow morning. God Bless America."

Jack went back to his barracks room to shower and change into one of the new tailored uniforms he had purchased. The Officers' Club would be crowded with men and women in a festive mood, and he wanted to share the occasion. When the guns become silent after six years of violence and bloodshed, it was cause to celebrate. Jack was not a heavy drinker, but he enjoyed an occasional beer and glass of wine. He began smoking a pipe when his therapy session started. All through college until he was taken captive on Bataan, he had enjoyed smoking one. He found the routine of cleaning, lighting and smoking to be therapeutic and satisfying. He was beginning to feel more like his old self and was pleased with the progress.

The hall was packed and the mood was buoyant, as he expected it to be. The dance floor was jammed with energetic couples. He made his way past the lounge to the dining room where he selected a full plate of roast beef and mashed potatoes from the large selections available at the buffet. The dining room was the quietest spot in the club. He chose a table near a window with a view of the harbor. Food was still a luxury for him. His taste for coffee was slow in developing, but it had arrived in full force as soon as he started to work out briskly. Always a heavy coffee drinker, he had to admit that the Navy made better coffee than the Army.

Ensign Kelly and another nurse from the hospital entered the Club and pushed their way through the crowd to the dining room for a lunch. They went through the serving line and looked for a place to sit. Ensign Kelly recognized Jack at one of the window tables.

"I see one of our old patients, Major Jack Ross," she declared to her friend. "What do you say if we join him?"

"I remember him. He was one of the POW's. Sure, why not? This place will soon be jammed full."

Jack saw the two nurses walking towards his table, and stood up to greet them. "Its been a while, Ensign Kelly."

"May we share your table? This is Ensign Talbert," introduced Ensign Kelly.

"Please sit down. It's my pleasure. I remember you from the hospital, Ensign Talbert. We have good news to celebrate for a change. The soldiers on both sides of the battlefield have much to be thankful for. Please make yourself comfortable and enjoy your meals. The roast beef is delicious and the coffee is first rate. I'm going up for another cup, may I get anything for either of you?"

"I could use a cup of coffee, Major," requested Ensign Kelly.

"I'm fine, Major, thanks," said Ensign Talbert.

Jack returned with the coffee. The crowd was beginning to get boisterous.

"I remember a story my father told me about the cease-fire order at the end of World War One on November eleventh at the eleventh hour," Jack related in a talkative mood. "He said the Germans, whom they had been trying to kill a few hours before, came out of their trenches to see what their former foes were doing. They were tired, haggard and frightened just like my father's platoon. The fact that all of them were hungry, and some needed medical attention, erased the bitterness and animosity toward the former enemy. The American lines were better supplied than the German defenders, so they were invited to come across 'no-man's land' to enjoy food, hot coffee, and receive the medical attention they needed. As the tattered and poorly dressed Germans came closer to the Allied trenches, the Americans recognized the same blank stares of soldiers who have seen too much death and destruction. In an instant, the Germans became an accepted part of the brotherhood of warriors, and they all celebrated the fact that they had survived the crucible. I never appreciated how my father must have felt at that time, but now I think I know what it must have been like. I've experienced a similar deliverance and am thankful just to be alive."

The nurses heard the story and saw the impact it had on Jack. Usually he was a loner who did not share his feelings or inner thoughts with others except for his close friends, whom he selected with care. Generally, he was sensitive and vulnerable and kept his own counsel.

"How are things at therapy?" asked Ensign Kelly.

"If you know Miss Patti, then you can imagine that she has us going wide open most of the time."

"I've heard of her," Ensign Talbert smiled knowingly. "She was the first native Hawaiian to be commissioned in any of the services."

"When I first met her my initial reaction was negative. I still harbor a special hatred of the Japanese that imprisoned me and murdered hundreds of my comrades. Miss Patti has made me see the wisdom of restricting my prejudice towards those who warrant the anger."

"Sounds like a wise concept," said Ensign Kelly, noting an improvement in the recovery of her former patient.

The air was resonating with energetic celebrations. The dining room was filled to capacity. Ensign Talbert announced that she was scheduled for an evening shift at the hospital, and said good-bye.

"Are you just getting off your shift, Ensign Kelly?" asked Jack, once they were alone.

"Yes, I'm finished for the day. It was a busy one. The hospital ship is getting ready for another trip to the southwest Pacific. I've been wondering if I should sign on again," she answered soberly.

"Where are you from, Ensign Kelly? I'm beginning to detect a slight New England accent in some of your expressions."

"I'm from a small town in upper state New York, Warrensburg. It's near Lake George."

"I've been to Lake George. It's a beautiful place. I went to an infantry school at Plattsburg before the war."

"That's north of Warrensburg on Lake Champlain."

"I'm from Wells, Maine, on the southern coast. I graduated from the University of New Hampshire at Durham which was close to Wells. We were almost neighbors," he laughed. "Do you have anything planned for the evening?"

"Are you asking me for a date, Major?" she asked directly.

"Yes, I guess I am," he admitted, surprised that he had asked the question. "I've heard a lot about Schofield Barracks, a few miles in the mountains from Pearl Harbor. The Navy motor pool has authorized me to use a sedan this evening to visit the place. Would you like to accompany me, unless you have something else planned…?"

"No, I don't have anything planned, Major," she answered. "We don't really know each other that well. It's a little irregular, but yes, I'll go up to Schofield Barracks with you. I've never been there either. It sounds like fun."

Ten minutes after they left the Officers' Club, Jack was behind the wheel of a 1942 Plymouth sedan climbing the meandering stretch of road leading into the mountain range north of Pearl City. The twelve mile climb was gradual and continuous, and the views in the dusk of the evening were spectacular. Pineapple and sugar cane fields dotted the landscape between the coastal plain and the mountain ranges.

The large Army base was relatively open at that stage of the war. The Tenth Army staff that was responsible for the planning and assault of Okinawa had recently used the base for their planning sessions. A small airfield was adjacent to the extensive lawn. The base was essentially a small city containing a school, library, and living quarters for a large contingent of soldiers. They passed through the gate and toured around the buildings. Many of the older cement barracks built as quadrangles were vacant. Jack turned the Plymouth into a parking area next to a magnificent lookout pavilion. He turned off the ignition key and looked out over the darkened naval base below. A few lights still shown through the wartime blackout.

"This is what I wanted to see," said Jack, getting out of the car and opening Ensign Kelly's door for her. "We can stretch our legs a little if you want. I've heard tell that after sunset this is one of the most beautiful panoramas on the island of Oahu."

"Yes," she exclaimed, falling in step beside him as they made their way to a bench seat positioned for maximum breadth of view.

"My father was in the Army for a few years after the First War. He was stationed here. I promised him that I'd check out the overview that he described as the best around."

"I'd say that it lives up to his description. You think a lot of your father, don't you?" she asked casually.

"I never knew my mother. She died giving me birth. My father and I were very close over the years. He became my best friend. I love and respect him. He tried to make up for her loss by sharing his memories of her with me. I hope that I can be half the man he has been," Jack replied, captivated by the half moon coming out of a low-lying cumulous cloud. The water in the harbor below glistened from the reflected moonbeams. How often he had watched a moon like that from his dark fetid hut and wondered if there was civilization beyond the jungles that surrounded them!

"The cool air feels good after being cooped up all day in a ward. It's a beautiful place," she exclaimed, watching the dark shapes within the harbor become more defined by the rays of the moon. "From here it's hard to imagine the horrors that took place on December seventh in 1941. I'm so thankful that the war in Europe is over. There has been enough killing and maiming of young bodies at the threshold of a full life," Ensign Kelly declared, striking a pensive pose.

Jack understood how a nurse must feel. They dealt with the full reality of what hot steel can do to soft flesh. "I notice that you still wear your wedding band in memory of your husband. I respect that." He looked at her and saw sadness in her eyes. "I'm sorry. I didn't mean to dredge up hurtful memories."

"I know, Major. I know that he's gone, but I haven't totally accepted that fact yet. I think I've been too long in denial. It's quiet, reflective moments like this that the truth starts to hurt the most. I never had a chance to say good-bye or ease his pain at the end...."

"You carry a burden of grief and loss that is being replicated thousands of times by families all over the country. I've admired your compassion and sensitivity to the patients in your care. You have a gift for making people with broken bodies feel better. I've respected that from the first day I woke up on the hospital ship and saw you with a dying soldier. Your courage in caring for those of us who needed it is an inspiration to everyone. I don't see how you've been able to do it and still carry the deep personal loss of your husband at the same time. I'm sure he looks upon your devotion with great pride."

"Thank you for the kind compliments, Major Ross. It's always nice to know that one is appreciated. I do my best and sometimes it's very difficult." She shivered when a damp breeze blew from the harbor.

"Here, I insist that you take this," demanded Jack, removing his Army jacket and placing it around her shoulders. "I'm dressed enough without it."

"It does feel good," she replied softly. "How long do you think it'll be before the Japanese surrender?"

"Within a year. They'll fight to the last man if we invade the home islands. There probably is no other way. The Army has told me that I will not be allowed back in combat for a while, so my active fighting days are over. I'll be going back to the mainland soon with a long furlough."

"What would you do if you left the Army?"

"I'm a graduate civil engineer. I specialized in design and construction of bridges. I've thought of resigning my commission. With things the way they are I'm not so sure about anything..."

"Have you heard from your wife?"

"No, and I don't expect to. I've talked to my father about the situation every time I call him. Nothing has changed. I'm not as angry about it as I was. I can understand how it came about, and your advice to blame the war has helped a lot. When I go home, I'll settle it and start to build a new life the best I can."

57

"It's possible that we won't see each other again. If that's the case, I want you to know that caring for you and the other former prisoners was something special," Ensign Kelly told him.

Jack heard what she was saying and turned to confront her. "We were all aware of that. I'm not an expert in affairs of the heart, and what I'm about to say may be out of line. My personal life is in so much chaos that I don't know where I want to go from here. I do know that I'd value a friend like you, Lorena. That's the first time I've called you Lorena. A pretty name for a pretty lady. Could we keep in touch and write once in a while?"

"We're two unsettled people right now, Jack. I imagine the world is full of individuals just like us trying to put their lives in order. The war has changed a lot of things. Echoes of the past are still very strong. I don't know what I want, but a friend is always a comfort. I like your suggestion. Respect and trust are two worthwhile virtues to build a friendship upon. Right now I need a friend more than I need a lover. I'm glad you asked me to come up here with you," Lorena replied softly.

"So am I. Can we seal our friendship with a kiss?"

Lorena answered by coming into his arms and lifting her lips to his. She rested her head on his shoulder feeling secure and no longer alone. "You may not believe it, but the first time I saw you lying on the bed of the hospital ship so pathetically worn out and alone, I had a premonition that you and I could share a friendship. Let's go on from here gaining strength and solace from that relationship. Maybe tomorrow, in another time and place there might be more… Tomorrow will have to take care of itself."

Chapter Seven

The physical therapy session for Jack was ending soon. Miss Patti was correct when she predicted that those who fulfilled the requirements of the regimen would be pleased with the results. Jack was happy with the amount of progress he had made since the Rangers escorted him to safety. His muscular frame was toned and vibrant. He had gained more than his original weight and lost two inches off his waist. Miss Patti was also responsible for increasing his lung capacity and endurance by introducing long distance running and jogging. Toward the end of the course, the vivacious Hawaiian nurse had the men eating out of her hand.

Most of the evenings and weekends were free for the men to do as they wished. Jack looked forward to seeing Lorena on evenings she could be free. They went bowling often and took in several movies. *Casablanca* was a favorite. Usually they ended the evenings of bowling or a movie with a stop at the Officers' Club where they enjoyed a light snack and a leisurely glass of wine to end the day's activities. Their relationship was relaxed and mutually rewarding. Each was aware that they could easily have crossed the line and been lovers, but they refrained from the temptation for fear of losing the friendship they both valued.

One night, after they saw *The Best Years of Our Lives*, they walked from the movie theater along the waterfront. The ships in the harbor were still black, their profile readily visible against the star-studded sky. The business establishments on the waterfront were bustling with merry soldiers, sailors and marines. The haunting strains of a Hawaiian steel guitar floated across the beach, echoing against the massive hulks in the harbor. Lorena was a little quieter than usual.

"Is there anything wrong, Lorena?" asked Jack, holding her hand.

"No, I've just been thinking a lot more about today and what tomorrow might bring," she replied reflectively. "It's getting along towards the end of May, and your therapy sessions will be coming to an end. I've been thinking about that, and I'll miss not having a friend around, that's all."

"These have been swell times, haven't they? The Army has supplied me with Combat Infantrymen's Badges and Purple Hearts for the seven families I've committed myself to visit. I want to make those visits as soon as possible. The families may not want to hear what I have to say, but I hope to impress upon each of them that courage and valor are displayed in places other than the battlefield."

"I'm sure you'll make the families feel better with your visit. It's a noble undertaking. I can't imagine how you men survived all those years," Lorena told him, shuddering at the thought.

"We did it by forming a very special brotherhood. It's hard to share the experience with anyone who was not there. Those who died left a legacy of hope, raw courage, and an appreciation of the inherent dignity of man that should be an inspiration to the rest of the world. I just want to tell their story so that they will never be forgotten." Jack felt passionately about the subject and his obligation to his dead comrades.

Lorena squeezed his hand. "I'm sure you will, Jack. Perhaps you need to do this for yourself as much as for the dead soldiers. I'm proud of you. You're a good man, Major Ross. Those soldiers that served under you were fortunate."

"I'm sure there are some who would disagree with you," he laughed shyly.

"I won't be going to sea again. I'm scheduled to attend a refresher training seminar at Kaneohe. I'll be leaving first thing in the morning. It's getting late, Jack, and I should get back to quarters."

"I'll walk you to the barracks," he offered, suddenly feeling sad. "I guess this is good-bye then."

"It had to come some day. I'll remember the times we've spent together with fondness. For a while, it was possible to forget the war and enjoy each other's company. I needed those periods of normalcy. I'll miss you, and I promise to keep in touch. I hope you can read my penmanship. It's really horrible," she chuckled, hiding the emotions that lurked just below the surface.

"I won't complain if you don't about mine." He held her hand. It was going to be more difficult to say good-bye than he anticipated. "You once mentioned that echoes of the past are a part of our lives that have to be dealt with. I agree. I can tell you with certainty that I'm more prepared to face the future, no matter what it brings, than I was before you and I became friends."

They stopped near the entrance to the nurses barracks. "I don't like good-byes," said Lorena impatiently. "They've had a habit of being too permanent. I'm relieved that you won't be going into combat. In a few days you'll be going home, and I wish you much happiness, Jack. Whatever takes place we can always be friends. I'm comforted by that. Thank you for being a gentleman and not asking for more."

"I'll try to make this as brief as I can, Lorena. We've been friends for a short period of time, yet it seems I've always known you. I guess it's not the longevity of friendship that counts as much as the intensity of involvement. I'll miss you, too. Promise me that if there is ever a time when you are in need of anything, without exception, that you'll call on me. Will you do that?"

"Yes, it's a promise made!"

"Good-bye, dear friend. You came into my life when I was a mere shell of a human being. How lucky I was to have you nurse me back to health. How does one say thank you for a life?"

"You already have by being yourself, Major Ross. Good-bye and good luck. May God walk with you." Lorena kissed him softly, then disappeared behind closed doors.

Jack watched her walk away and felt nakedly alone and abandoned. A cool breeze swept across the harbor. He turned to the shadowy figures of ships at anchor, hoping to capture the moment she said good-bye. He saw the tears in her eyes as she freed herself from his embrace. He scanned the water one more time and turned to leave, uncertain if his feelings were honest or simply a product of the turbulent war years he and Lorena had experienced.

Two days later, Jack left Pearl Harbor on a military transport plane bound for San Francisco. As the plane circled above the harbor he could see the Naval Hospital and the nurses barracks nearby. The emptiness he felt leaving Lorena was still with him. The extended furlough he was granted was welcome, but the concept of returning home filled him with apprehension and uncertainty, and no small amount of anger. In contrast, Lorena had asked for nothing from him, and gave freely of herself. He admired her for that unselfish commitment that seemed to be a common attribute of nurses everywhere.

His flight plans called for a delay at San Diego of an hour. He used the time to call his father.

"Hello, Dad."

"It's nice to hear your voice, Son."

"I'm on my way home. I'm at San Diego now. I'll pick up a flight from here to Boston and get a bus out of Boston to Wells. It's 2:00 PM here so it's 5:00 PM at Wells. I don't know when I'll arrive there."

"Whatever time it is, Son, I'll be glad to see you. It's been a long time."

"Possibly tomorrow before noontime. I'll be able to sleep on the plane. It seems that every time I call you, we talk about my problems. How are you doing, Dad?"

"I've come through the war years okay, Son. I'm getting older, but you know how it is. We keep getting better with age like good wine," his father chuckled.

"You haven't changed, Dad. Maybe I can give you a hand around the house or on some of your painting projects. We'll talk more when we get together. It's nice to be homeward bound. Thanks for being there for me, Dad."

"What else can a dad do? We'll celebrate when you get home."

"See you tomorrow. I love you."

"Love you too, Son."

The Boston Park Street bus station was jammed with humanity. Jack picked his way through the crowd to the ticket window and asked for a ticket to Wells, Maine on the Boston and Maine Bus Line.

"You're lucky, Major. There's a Boston and Maine bus at bay six ready to leave," the agent pointed out the location.

"I'll take it. I haven't been home in four years."

"Welcome home, soldier. Here's the ticket. There's no charge for returning soldiers. Good luck."

"Thank you, Sir."

Jack boarded the bus and settled in for the last leg of his journey back home. It would be a familiar ride back to Wells. He had already established some short term goals for himself. The first, and most urgent, was a meeting with Myla. He had no preconceived notions of what that confrontation would produce. He would have to see what developed. Another important goal was the visits to the seven families of his dead comrades. There was an urgency and a priority to that goal, regardless of what took place with Myla. Once that had been accomplished, then he could concentrate on the future. He thought of Lorena and how she would be proud of the way he was taking control of his life again.

The family homestead was located on U.S. Highway Route One. The Boston and Maine bus dropped him in front of the house. Jack's father was sitting on the front porch with his eyes riveted on the road leading from Ogunquit. The second he saw the familiar brown and tan B&M bus slow and pull off the road, he knew that his son had come home. He started to run down the driveway. Jack met him halfway, picking him up and swinging him around.

Isaac Ross was a modest, hard-working man. Thin and wiry, he was patient and reserved in everything he did. His alert eyes rarely missed anything around him. He took good care of himself and the home he had lived in for fifty years.

Orderly and meticulous, he was a little bit of a neat freak, and his son was the joy of his life. Father and son were a happy pair. Jack thought his father had aged. His hair was white and a few more lines were drawn beneath his eyes, but other than that, he was as chipper as ever!

"I've dreamed so often of home," Jack exclaimed, walking up the driveway with one arm around his father and the other carrying his large duffel bag.

They sat at the kitchen table eating ham sandwiches and drinking coffee for a couple of hours. Jack's father described in detail what Myla had gone through and how he viewed her decision to marry Jeff, an old friend from high school days. After hearing his Dad's explanation, Jack still blamed Myla.

"I'm not going to defend Myla, and I can't tell you how you should feel about what has taken place, Son. However, I have not looked upon her conduct or actions with the same animosity that you do. She's been very good to me. We've talked for hours about everything. She's still like a daughter to me, and I refuse to put her down. It's unfortunate and hurtful to all concerned, but there are no bad guys to blame here. The damned war is at fault!"

"Someone else told me the same thing, Dad. May I borrow your pickup truck? I want to see Myla. I could catch her at the school before she leaves. I would just as soon meet her at a neutral place for the first time."

"That sounds fair, Son. Here are the keys to the truck. It hasn't been started for a couple of days, so you'll have to choke it and pump it a few times."

"Thanks, Dad. I'll be back later. This is something I have to do."

"I understand, Son, but let me caution you. Don't let your anger rule you."

"I promise, Dad."

Myla had dismissed the fifth grade students with a sigh of relief. She was not herself, and had been snappy and impatient with the children throughout the day. She was angry that her personal affairs were affecting her relationship with the students. It had all started when Pops Ross called to tell her that

Jack was alive. Myla had also received a letter from the Army confirming that he had been a prisoner of war for three and a half years. She prayed for strength to stop by the house to see Jack. She was anxious to see him and frightened at the same time. Pops had told her that he was extremely angry at her.

Myla knew that Jack had been in a prison camp until he was rescued by American forces invading the Philippines the evening before she had received another call from Pops that Jack was on his way home. She expected him to appear at the school anytime, and watched the door whenever it was opened and kept an eye on the parking lot outside. Her main concern was he might try to visit her while the children were in the classroom.

Just getting through the day was an accomplishment for Myla. Now that the room was quiet she took a seat near the front of the classroom, feeling weak and uncertain about herself. She had done a monstrous thing. She had married an old friend of Jack's, Jeff Snow. She rationally went through the reasons leading up to the decision to marry Jeff.

The last letter Myla had received from Jack was postmarked February 27, 1942. The letters she had written to him dated after New Year of 1942, were returned to her with a notice of "Return to Sender, Address Unknown." On April 1, 1942, the Army had notified her that Jack was missing in action and presumed dead. Two months later, an Army Lieutenant visited her with information that the International Red Cross had searched all of the prisoner-of-war camps in the Philippines and were unable to locate her husband, and the Army could not find any record of his presence in the guerrilla groups in the mountains of Luzon. The young lieutenant had turned over Jack's battered dog tag that had been found on Bataan. The Army had exhausted their resources to locate her husband and had declared him as killed-in-action instead of missing. That was July 4, 1942. Myla had no way of knowing with certainty that her Jack was alive. The war years had not been easy for her. She was a widow having difficulty making ends meet with her salary as a teacher. Now that Jack was home, the tragic consequences of her actions overwhelmed her.

Jack drove his father's Ford pickup truck into the elementary school parking lot near the center of town. His recovery had surprised him, and he was glad that Myla never saw him when he first left the prison camp. His new tailored uniforms fit as if he had been poured into them. He was nervous turning off the ignition key. His mind was a blank. The children and the rest of the faculty had already left the school. The only automobile in the parking lot was a Pontiac that he recognized as belonging to Myla's mother. That suited him fine. He was anxious to see Myla, but did not want to create a scene. He had dreamed of her every day and night for the past three and a half years. She was very likely responsible for his still being alive. Their love for each other had been his greatest inspiration during those dark, long years in the foul-smelling jungles. His love for her remained the same. Jack quietly opened the door for the fifth grade classroom. He saw Myla sitting in one of the desks near the blackboard holding her head in her two hands. He could not believe that he was home and Myla was in the same room with him. Her thick auburn hair was cut short just beneath her ears. She was like an apparition from heaven to him. Those who knew her well called her a loyal friend and a good listener who rarely passed judgment unless asked to do so. She had dark green eyes and black eyebrows with prominent high cheek bones covered with a few freckles. To some she was beautiful, but most regarded her as cute. She could be demanding of her students who admired her for her fairness and commitment to their welfare. The community liked her, and she lived a quiet, somewhat reclusive private life.

Having come this far, Jack was uncertain what to say or do in her presence. His heart was beating wildly. It was difficult controlling an urge to run and sweep her up in his arms. He was filled with shock, anger and a sense of having been betrayed that his wife could not wait for the war to end before marrying again. He cleared his throat to speak to her.

"Is that you, Myla?"

She turned and saw him standing in the doorway holding his hat in his hand. There had always been a strong presence about him. He was serious and studious by nature, but at times he could laugh and joke like a little boy. It had been easy to love him. At first glance, he looked the same in his uniform. He was still a handsome man, but as she looked closer, Myla realized that he was not the same person she had kissed and sent off to war. His black hair was heavily speckled with gray even though he was only twenty-eight years old. Three years of imprisonment were mirrored in his penetrating gray eyes that looked through her. The deep recess of his eye sockets had not disappeared.

"Jack," she cried with alarm. "I hardly recognized you. What have I done to us?"

"That's what I came to see you about, Myla. I'm at a loss for words right now. I think you owe me an explanation that I can believe." He felt victimized and angry that he could not hold her and that their love had not been strong enough. She had discarded the love they shared for most of their lives. "I understand that the Army had me listed as missing and then as deceased."

"That's true, Jack, and when I received the news I refused to accept it. Then months and years went by with no word from you or the Army. Those were long years for me, Jack. I'm not trying to make excuses for my actions, but I had to ultimately accept the fact that you were never coming home. I was sick with despair, and even your Dad was worried about my sanity and health. I remained true to our memories for a long time."

"I thought Jeff was in the Navy."

"He was wounded somewhere in the Pacific and lost part of his arm. He has an artificial limb now and has adapted to it very well. When he was discharged from the Navy we talked a lot about the war and became good friends. We got married the first of the year. He's been good to me...."

"I see," replied Jack, wanting to run away and not let her see how much it all hurt. The ugly thought of her with another man, even an old friend, was ripping him apart. When his father told him about Jeff and Myla, it was as if he had been physically assaulted and he did not know how to handle it.

Myla saw the pain and anguish in him and reached out to comfort him. He pulled away from her and turned to leave. He had heard enough for one day. He hesitated at the door.

"Dad told me that you had something important to tell me. He refused to say what it was about, so I'm asking you. Is there anything else that I should know that you haven't told me?"

Myla wiped the tears from her red eyes and walked towards him. "I never had a chance to tell you, Jack. We have a daughter."

Chapter Eight

"My daughter or Jeff's?" asked Jack contemptuously.

Myla slapped him hard across the face. The sound echoed within the classroom. He regretted the choice of words the minute he blurted it out.

"How dare you accuse me of that. I understand that all of this has hurt you deeply, Jack. That still doesn't give you the right to make crude accusations about my faithfulness to you," she cried aloud, angered and feeling helpless. "I'll never be able to comprehend the horror you went through, but I can tell you from experience that it was hell being here with our child and the knowledge that you were not coming home and would never know her. Soldiers are not the only ones who had to fight this war. Daily life was an uphill struggle for me for years. I'm not complaining; I simply want you to know how it really was."

"I'm sorry, it was unfair of me."

"You're right, Jack. It was so uncharacteristic of you to reach out and hurt people with words you don't mean. My God in Heaven, it hurts to be standing here in front of you verbally battling when I so badly want to take you in my arms and say I'm sorry. To have you look at me the way you are now filled with hate and scorn is painful. I can understand why you would feel that way, but it's unfair… it's unfair… Now please leave, I don't want you to see me this way…"

Jack turned on his heel and left the classroom as fast as he could. He sat in the pickup truck and bawled like a baby. This wasn't the homecoming he had dreamed about.

Pops Ross watched the truck turn into the driveway. One look at his son told him that things did not go well. He sighed and asked the Lord to help him. He loved his son more than life itself and had loved Myla as the daughter he never had. Their daughter Roselyn was a precious gift from Heaven. Jack came into the house radiating the turmoil that filled him. He wanted to comfort his Son but didn't know how.

"You never told me about the baby, Dad."

"Under the circumstances I gave in to Myla's wishes. She wanted to be the one to tell you about your daughter. Her name is Roselyn."

"Roselyn!" exclaimed Jack.

"That's right. Myla wanted her to be named in memory of your mother. Naturally I was pleased. She's a beautiful child and Myla is a wonderful mother. I'm sure that your mother watches over her namesake as a guardian angel. One of the reasons I see Myla so much is because of Roselyn. I can't tell you what a joy she has been to my life. Whatever you do, Jack, don't shut that child out of your life. Myla was pregnant with her even before the end of your last furlough."

"I questioned if the child was mine or Jeff's," admitted Jack, ashamed of the admission.

"It's not like you to be vindictive and mean. Myla didn't deserve that."

"I know that now, Dad. I wasn't thinking straight."

They spent the next hour talking about his daughter and the way things had been during the war. His father looked out the window and announced, "I see Myla driving in the yard."

Jack looked and saw the 1941 Nash Ambassador he and Myla had purchased before the war pull to a stop in the driveway. It looked as good as new. Myla left the driver's seat and went around to the passenger side to help a little girl dressed in a pair of red jumpers and a red sweatshirt. Jack's heart started pounding when he saw his daughter for the first time. He wasn't prepared for this and grasped a chair to steady himself.

Pops Ross opened the kitchen door and walked out on the porch to meet them. The little girl ran into his open arms. She wrapped her arms around his neck tightly and looked at the tall soldier behind her "Grandpops". Myla held back, hesitant about entering the house.

"Please come in, Myla. Do you recognize the soldier, Roselyn?"

"He's the man in the picture," she answered, staring at him with her bright blue-green eyes and still clinging tightly to her Grandpops.

"That's your Daddy, Honey," said Myla, wiping a curl away from her eye. She turned and looked directly at Jack standing in the door. "Ever since she was born, I kept a picture of you and I on the stand next to her bed. It was one of the pictures taken of us at the cottage the last time we were together. The picture was the last thing she saw before going to sleep and the first thing she saw upon waking in the morning. I wanted her to remember her father the way he was when we last saw him."

"I don't know what to say..." confessed Jack. He held out his hands to little Roselyn. She reacted by hanging tighter to her Grandpops. "I guess she's afraid of me."

"She's at that stage a lot of children go through where they're cautious of strangers. It'll take some time," said Myla, holding a set of keys out to Jack. "I thought you would need transportation so I took the Nash out of storage. I haven't used it for a couple of years. These are the keys. The key to the cottage is also on the ring. It's been vacant for the past two years. I'm living in town within walking distance to the school. You'll find the cottage much the same as you remember it except for the papering and painting inside. I've got to go now. There's a Parent-Teacher meeting at the school tonight. One of the other teachers is waiting to pick me up. Your Dad offered to watch Rose for a couple of hours. Don't be afraid of her, Jack. She's just a little girl and no matter what you think of me, she'll always be your daughter."

"Thanks for the keys to the Nash," replied Jack soberly. "I apologize for the words I used earlier. I didn't really mean to strike out like that."

"I accept your apology. Thanks for being so helpful, Pops. I'll be back within a couple of hours."

"You know it's a pleasure."

Myla ran out the door past Jack to a waiting automobile at the end of the driveway.

"Well, Son, this is as good a time as any to get acquainted with your daughter. Are you hungry, Rose?"

Rose answered with a shy, "Yes," all the time heeding the tall man Grandpops called her Daddy.

"I see your mother brought along some coloring books and crayons. Now you can show us how well you can color." Grandpops picked her up to place her in an elevated chair at the head of the table where the books and crayons were located.

"Mommy tells me to be careful when I color to not go over the lines." Jack ran his fingers through her rich auburn hair. She had Myla's blue-green eyes and hair color. He picked up one of her hands and marveled at the perfect tiny fingers, soft and delicate. He thought she was the most precious being he had ever seen. She looked up at him and half smiled as if to say that she wanted to be friends but she was being cautious. In that instant, she had won the heart of her daddy the way little girls have been doing since the world began.

"Grandpops says I color good."

"I'll bet Grandpops is correct," Jack answered. She had completely captivated his father, and Jack had never seen him happier than he was caring for his little granddaughter.

"She's a gem, Jack. As you can tell, she has Myla's hair and eyes, and she's got your nose and mouth. Frequently, when her mother drops her off, we share a peanut butter and marshmallow fluff sandwich with a glass of milk, heavy to fluff or it sticks to the roof of your mouth too much. She's a good eater, but she fights going to bed sometimes. Mommy wins that contest every time. When she comes to Grandpops' house now, little Rose doesn't have to use diapers anymore. She has grown up and uses the bathroom just like a big girl, except we have a small training chair for her exclusive use in the bathroom. We're really proud of her for making that adjustment so well."

Rose colored a picture of a monkey climbing a palm tree. The monkey was brown, the tree was green and the sky was light blue. Rose showed it to Jack for his approval while Grandpops was busy fixing a sandwich on the kitchen counter.

"That's very good, Roselyn. Your name is the same as my mother. It's a nice name."

"Yes, she's Grandmom and she's in Heaven. Was you in Heaven with her?" asked Rose. Jack looked at his father.

"You know, Son, Rose had to be told something about her Daddy. We never knew…"

"I know, Dad," Jack answered, shrugging his shoulders. "No, I wasn't in Heaven with your Grandmom, Honey. Someday when you're older, your Daddy will tell you about it." It was the first time he had referred to himself as "Daddy". It made him feel warm all over. "Your coloring of a monkey is very much like the real monkeys. Daddy was on an island where there were a lot of monkeys. They make funny sounds when they talk to each other in the trees." Jack puckered his lips and tried to imitate some of the sounds he remembered so well. Rose laughed at him and with him. The bond had been established!

"Okay gang, eating is serious business. Here come the sandwiches and ice cold milk to wash them down," proclaimed Grandpops, placing a plate of sandwiches on the table.

The next two hours went quickly. Jack's father had accumulated a box of miscellaneous toys that he kept in a closet in the living room. Rose asked him if she could play with some of the toys in the box. He gladly complied and emptied it in the middle of the living room floor. Building blocks, coloring books and an assortment of dolls and Teddie bears were scattered about.

"Which one is your favorite toy?" asked Jack, sitting on the floor with her. Rose picked up a brown bear with a red ribbon around its neck and hugged it. "Why is that your favorite toy?" he asked to test her.

"Because he is soft and fussy," she answered, surprised that he didn't know that already! They laughed together again. It felt good.

Jack assembled a couple of dozen building blocks placing them on top of each other. He was serious and very quiet while building the tower of blocks, holding a finger up to his lips for her to be quiet. Rose understood and watched with intense focus as he continued building the block tower taller and taller. Jack placed each succeeding block on top of the last one with great precision and flourish. Rose was mesmerized. The tower grew to three feet tall, positioned between Jack and Rose. He once again admonished her to remain quiet and placed a few more blocks on the tower.

Suddenly, Jack let out a loud yell and hit the base of the tower with his hand as if he was making a Karate chop. The blocks scattered all over the floor. Rose was startled and jumped when he cried out and began laughing as the tower was demolished. She laughed and clapped her hands at the crazy thing he did. They rebuilt the tower several times before Myla showed up.

She closed the door behind her and watched Jack and Rose knock the block tower down with shrieks of laughter. Jack was as happy as Rose. She turned away from them and ran to Pops Ross in the kitchen. Her lips were trembling. She was fighting to hold back the tears but lost the battle. Pops took her into his arms. "It's a sight to gladden the heart, isn't it, Myla?" She nodded her head in agreement.

"I never thought I'd see the day when little Rose could play with her father."

Jack heard her voice and stood up to acknowledge her. "I didn't hear you come in."

Rose ran to her mother and clasped her arms around her legs. She saw that her mother had been crying. "Don't cry Mommy, don't cry. Daddy is not in Heaven."

"I know that now, Honey. I didn't know that until he came home."

"She's a beautiful child. You've done a great job with her, Myla. I wish I could have known about her. A bundle of joy has suddenly come into my life. I don't know what to say," Jack exclaimed.

"I wish you could have known about her too, Jack. I wrote a lot of letters to you, but they all came back with 'Return To Sender' on them. It was nice to see that you two got along so well on your first visit," Myla said, avoiding Jack's troubled expression. "Honey, we've got to leave. Mrs. Lane is waiting in the car for us. The toys have got to be picked up and placed back in the closet before we leave."

"Since I made some of the mess, it's only fair that I help. Here's your favorite Teddie bear," added Jack, getting down on his knees to help. He passed the bear to Roselyn. "It's nice and fuzzy," he grinned.

They cleaned up the contents of the box, and Jack helped Rose carry it to the closet. She then ran to Grandpops and gave him a hug and kiss and did the same to Jack as if they had been friends for a long time. "Good night, Daddy."

"Good night, Roselyn."

Myla grabbed her by the hand and thanked Jack and his father for taking care of Rose. She ran with her to the waiting car. He and his father watched them leave.

"It's been an eventful day, Dad. I know that it's late, but I'm going to take the Nash out for a ride to the cottage. I couldn't sleep anyway. Maybe I'll stay there for the night. I'm not sure. There are so many things running through my head right now, I need a chance to sort them out. I'll be back to have breakfast with you."

"It's nice to have you back. The main switch at the cottage has been closed. Myla goes out there to air it out every once in a while. I wish I could help you resolve what seems to be unsolvable."

"Dad, you've always helped me the most by just being yourself. My daughter loves you. I've heard it said that children have an unerring knack of trusting people that can be trusted. I'm glad that she has brightened your life. It was nice to see that. Don't worry about me, I'll be all right, you'll see."

"Good night, Son."

Jack re-familiarized himself with the controls of the Nash. It was nice to get behind the wheel. It still had the clean smell of a new car. He started the smooth running overhead valve six cylinder engine. It was quiet and responsive. It felt natural to be driving it again as he headed toward the coastal road to Kennebunkport. The long driveway to the cottage on the rocky shore was just like he remembered it. He had dreamed often about returning. The cottage had been a refuge for him, a sanctuary where he was king of the domain. The day he and Myla signed for the mortgage was one of the happiest of his life. The headlights of the Nash picked up the cottage perched on a rocky promontory surrounded on three sides by the cold waters of the Atlantic Ocean. It was a Cape Cod type with two dormers facing the ocean. The gray weathered shingles contrasted with the white trim around the windows and doors. He unlocked the door and felt along the wall until he came to a steel fuse box. He lit a match to see where the master switch was located and tripped it. The lights came on over the kitchen sink. Lorena's remark about echoes from the past ran through his mind. The cottage wreaked of memories of better times.

He had finally come home. He turned the lights on in every room to see what had changed. Most of the walls had been newly covered with sheetrock and painted or wallpapered. When he left for overseas duty, the only thing that had been done to the interior was insulation of the walls. The largest room in the cottage was called the den. It had the best views of the ocean with a picture window near the center of the room.

A small room off the den was located against the side of the house facing the driveway. It was an empty area when he was home last. Myla had it finished in native knotty white pine paneling and had installed a floor to ceiling bookcase against one of the walls. The case was filled with books he and Myla had packed away in boxes when they graduated from college. He checked closely and noted that all of his college engineering textbooks were neatly arranged on a single shelf. He also noticed a familiar old desk in the corner of the room which could properly have been called a study. The desk was the one he had as a little boy and a young man from his father's house. His dad must have brought it over to Myla.

Jack placed his reading glasses on and turned on a small lamp on the desk so that he could review the large stack of material. Newspaper clippings, articles from magazines, *National Geographic* magazine, and pamphlets all pertaining to the Philippine Island Campaign had been assembled there. There was a large detailed daily chronicle of events on Luzon, the Bataan Peninsula and Corregidor, the large island off the coast of Bataan.

A voluminous file of letters sent to and from the International Red Cross Agency were also in the desk. Evidently Myla had left no stone unturned in her search to locate him or determine if he was dead or alive. She had also requested information and asked questions of every senator and representative from Maine and New Hampshire regarding the truthfulness of his death as the Army had presented it to her. He was impressed by the sheer volume of information she had collected. A map of the Philippines was attached to the pine paneling. Dotted lines and colored shaded areas followed the Japanese advances through the island. The exact same routes of invasion were used in 1944 by the Sixth Army under General Walter Krueger. Myla's last entry was a note of the January 6, 1945 landing at Lingayen Gulf.

The compact student's desk had three small drawers on the left side where he had kept his school supplies. He opened them and found that Myla had filled them with all of the photographs they had taken since they first started grade school together. They were sorted by periods. On the top were the most recent pictures taken at the cottage just before he had left. He reminisced with several photos before placing them back in their envelopes and closing the drawer. He removed his glasses and wiped his eyes free of moisture. The pictures were difficult to look at. It represented a time and place that no longer existed. Thoughts of what might have been were painful to contemplate. He recalled "echoes of the past" once again.

Stretching out on the comfortable lounge in the den with a wide view of the ocean, Jack laid his head against the pillowed backrest and watched a brilliant half moon rise out of the tumbling waves. The restless energy of the water breaking against the fragmented rocks soothed his troubled soul. It was a peaceful scene where he had once felt tranquility and unity with himself and those around him. Part of his unrest and discontent was that the more he searched for that same level of serenity, the more disjointed his life seemed to become. The world had turned around many times since he and Myla had sat on the same lounge locked in each other's arms. In that time and place they didn't need anything else to make their lives complete. A part of his life had been taken away from him, and he mourned its loss.

Jack recalled something Sergeant Buxton had told him one evening in the darkness of their hut in the prison camp just days before he died: "You know, Captain, every man has his own way of holding on to that thin thread of normalcy which keeps us from joining those who've gone over the edge. Every night I dream of home, placid waters, clean sheets and perfumed women. Right now I'd settle for a juicy steak and a glass of cold milk." Memories of the fearless Sergeant Buxton helped Jack align his priorities. He decided to start out in the morning to visit the soldiers' families. Having the Nash made the decision a lot easier.

Personal problems could be placed on hold. Jack did not deceive himself that solutions were not on the immediate horizon. Once he made that decision, he closed his eyes and fell asleep, remembering courageous acts that the world should never forget. He woke with the appearance of the first rays of sunshine rising in the east above the water and entering the room. He yawned and checked his watch. It was 6:30 AM. He needed a shave and coffee and prepared to leave for his father's house. The water was turned off in the cottage, and he did not want to disturb that just now. He made sure all of the doors were locked and lights turned off, and walked towards the waiting Nash. Crisp air carried across the pulsating waves of the water, filling his lungs. He breathed deeply of the freshness of the sea.

Just as he reached for the door, Myla pulled up behind the Nash with her mother's Pontiac. "I thought you might be here," she said, getting out of the car. "I wanted to talk to you about something."

"That's interesting, because I had a chance last night to think a lot about things and have arrived at a decision. Our marital status is somewhat embarrassing now. I want you to know that I'm on my way to see a lawyer about a divorce or an annulment or whatever is needed for us to become disentangled. That way our status will at least be legal."

A look of disbelief came over her. "If that's what you want, Jack. I came here to the cottage expecting to find you. I was going to suggest a way that would be the best for everybody concerned, especially Roselyn, but your determination seems clear enough. I'm sorry I stopped by, you've already made up your mind."

"There was a time, Myla, when we could read each other's thoughts and complete each other's sentences. I hope you're happy in your new life. Tell me the truth. Are you happy?"

"Happiness is a word with many meanings, Jack. Do you mean am I happy like you and I were at one time? The answer is no. That was a long time ago. People and situations change, and the war changed everyone's lives forever. We're all victims, and each person has to make decisions on the basis of circumstances that exist at that time. Is your plan to resolve the situation a final one, Jack? Is that what you really want?"

"What I want doesn't seem to matter anymore, Myla. You made a choice with Jeff. I had no part in that decision. If you have anything else in mind, I'd like to hear it," Jack replied, holding the pain and disappointment inside. He filled his pipe and held a match to the tobacco in the bowl, all the time watching Myla. She was having difficulty maintaining self-control.

"Jack," she said in a low voice, biting her lip to keep from crying in front of him. "Whatever you decide is acceptable to me. Your suggestion seems to be correct and legal. I just don't know anymore! Roselyn is your daughter, and I have never denied that to her."

"I thank you for that small favor. I hope that I can do my share as her father."

"I knew you'd agree with that. Roselyn was the single life-line that maintained my sanity for most of the war because she needed me. Believe me, I needed her more." Myla broke down and started to cry. "So, I guess we've solved the problems. I've got to get to the school. The first bus will be arriving soon."

"Who takes care of Roselyn?"

"My mother," answered Myla, starting the Pontiac.

Jack wanted to end the conversation on a civil note. "The cottage looks great. You did a nice job on it, Myla."

"It's just a cottage now. There was a time when it was a home…"

Chapter Nine

"We agree on that, Myla," Jack called out to her as she backed the Pontiac out of the driveway.

She was upset and refused to look at him. Jack was sure that she was crying. He had a strong urge to take her in his arms the way he had often done, but pride got in his way. He stood there in the driveway trying to piece together what she really came for. Was it to seek some kind of truce? For a split second he had a feeling that she was going to offer a reconciliation. He thought long and hard on that prospect, and his heart beat faster; then, he thought of her quick agreement to his divorce or annulment proposal and dismissed the idea. She had conceded to his plan without a counter offer. As far as he was concerned, the route he had laid out was crystal clear and met with her approval.

Hours later, Jack was driving the Nash north toward the Moosehead Lake region of Maine. His first stop was the home of the parents of his friend, Sergeant Eddie Buxton. They lived in the small, rural town of Abbot, a few miles south of Moosehead Lake. Jack had called ahead for reservations in a hotel on Moosehead at Greenville. He arrived at the small town of Abbot at 1:00 PM, right after lunch, intentionally planning it that way so that the family would not feel obligated to prepare something for him to eat.

He turned off the main road in a westerly direction and drove about five miles. The modest two-story home with a high pitched roof to shed the heavy snow loads that were normal for the area was much as Buxton had described it to Jack. They were further north than the city of Montreal, and the winters were severe and long. The white clapboard house with an attached barn was neat and orderly. A small section of lawn had been recently mowed. The sweet smell of curing grass filled the brisk air. Several cords of cut and split hardwood firewood were piled along the side of the driveway and against the small shed at the rear of the house where it would cure and dry over the summer months before being used in the fall and winter.

Jack knocked on the door and was met by a middle-aged man with a medium build, dark hair, and sad eyes. He greeted Jack with a firm handshake and graciously invited him to come inside the house. Jack noticed a gold star hanging in the window on the door beneath a picture of their son. Jack self-consciously removed his hat as he entered the house. An air of dark apprehension permeated the home.

"My wife and I have been expecting you," said James Buxton, with some uncertainty, leading him into a large country kitchen not unlike the one Jack grew up in. Sergeant Eddie Buxton looked like his father. A beige-colored cast iron stove took up one corner of the kitchen. A coffee pot was percolating on the front firebox section. "We'll be more comfortable here at the table."

"This will be fine, Mr. Buxton."

A short portly woman in her early forties with rosy red cheeks and graying hair came out from a pantry beside the kitchen with a tray of homemade donuts and placed them on the table. Jack saw the despair and pain in her eyes, even though she tried to be a cheerful hostess.

"Major Ross, this is Ed's mother, Maude. Mom, this was Ed's commanding officer, Major Ross," Mr. Buxton introduced them in a shaking voice.

"I'm pleased to meet you, Mrs. Buxton."

"We've been looking forward to your visit ever since your call, Major. Please make yourself comfortable. Are you a coffee drinker?"

"I confess, I'm an addict," he said, smiling at the bereaved mother. It seemed to make her feel good that she could do something. He felt comfortable in the room.

Mr. Buxton was nervously folding his hands. He had large horny fingers that fidgeted a lot, manifesting a nervousness that Jack felt when he first met the man.

"Was you with our son when he died, Major?" asked Mr. Buxton in a beseeching tone of voice, unable to hold his tongue any longer. His wife quietly served coffee.

"Yes, I was, Mr. Buxton. Your son passed away in the middle of the night. I was at his side when he quietly closed his eyes for the last time and simply went to sleep. His passing was made with great expectation on his part. I believe that it was welcome. He was very sick with malaria, beriberi, and other tropical diseases. His last words in this life were 'Joyce'. He called out the name two times."

"Joyce was his fiancée," added Mrs. Buxton, placing a donut on a plate in front of him.

"Thank you, Mrs. Buxton, I haven't had a homemade donut in years. It'll be a treat."

"Why didn't we hear from the Red Cross?" Mr. Buxton asked nervously. He was wearing a pair of dungaree coveralls and continued to fidget with the metal buttons on the bib.

"I don't know, Sir. Neither the Red Cross nor the Allied Intelligence organizations were aware of the prison compound where we were detained. My father and wife believed me to be dead. I understand that the Army has sent you notification of his death and burial place."

"We received that just a few days ago, Major." It was difficult for Ed's father to talk about their deceased son. He restrained himself in front of Jack, but it was all he could do to keep from breaking down completely. Their only son was never coming home. Jack had wondered how he, personally, would handle such a calamity and questioned the value of the visit. Mrs. Buxton was a model of grace and understanding. She did not hold back the tears as well as her husband. They sprang from deep within her being and reached a crescendo that filled the room with agonizing sobs. Her husband rubbed her back and shoulders trying to console her. He bore his grief in silence looking on helplessly. There was nothing he could do to relieve their sorrow.

"Please, don't hold back on my account," Jack counseled in a soft voice. "I share your grief." Several minutes passed until the emotion-chocked room became silent. Then he began his story.

"The prison camp we were in was basically a slave labor holding center of several hundred men. We tended sugar cane and sugar beet fields all by hand. It was grueling work, and we were undernourished. Ed was a wonderful person. He constantly made fun of the guards and camp commander even at the risk of being severely punished." Jack told them about the flag incident and how it raised the spirits of the entire camp. He could not bring himself to elaborate on the severe beatings that ultimately ended in their son's death. They were carrying enough hurt. The cruel truth could only add to their misery, and Jack was unwilling to contribute to their sorrow.

"I can tell you," Jack continued in a reassuring manner. "Most of the inmates who died at the prison died because they wanted to. Death was welcomed as a release of the drudgery and misery that filled the days. Each hut functioned as a self-governing body. Ed was in my hut, and I was the senior officer. We slept next to each other for three and a half years. He often talked about both of you. His love for you and the precious memories he had of better times helped sustain him for the long ordeal of prison life.

"Ed's fondest memory which he often talked about were the times when the three of you went ice fishing on Lake Hebron with the bob-house. He was especially excited remembering when he had caught a large lake salmon. He also shared with me several of your berry-picking trips in some of the forest cut-over areas when he was a small boy. He laughed one night telling us about the time he got sick when he gorged himself on juicy red raspberries even though both of you had warned him not to over eat."

"I remember that time," said Mrs. Buxton, warmed by the memories of better days.

"When Ed was a little boy he loved to collect things, so berry-picking time appealed to him. I remember we used to make it a family affair and packed a lunch into some of the recent cut-over areas around town. Raspberries grew prolifically in newly open areas until other vegetation started competing for the space. God, it seems like yesterday," cried James Buxton.

"I want to impress upon you two that the days we spent in the prison compound were difficult, but the Japanese could never suppress the spirit of independence that was a large part of who your son was. When we were fighting on Bataan, he handled the platoon with firmness and fairness. The men liked him and looked up to him and would have followed him anywhere. On our last day of fighting on Bataan, Ed wanted to take off into the mountains to fight the Japanese as guerrillas. I wanted to do that too, but we had too many wounded men. If we had abandoned them to the Japanese, they would have been killed outright. We took the wounded men into captivity with us. Ed helped care for them. He had a very caring and generous side to him that became more apparent as time went by."

"You're right, Major," said Mrs. Buxton. "He was such a good boy to his Papa and me. I miss him terribly. A night never goes by that I don't send prayers for him to be at peace."

"I'm sure that your prayers are answered, Mrs. Buxton. He died peacefully. I can assure you of that. I've been authorized by the Army to leave this packet with you." Jack opened a wooden box and placed it on the table. "It contains a citation for a Purple Heart, the Purple Heart Medal and the Combat Infantryman's Badge, which Ed truly earned. He would have been proud to wear it. It's the most respected and coveted badge in the United States Armed Services."

"I've heard about the Combat Infantryman's Badge. I fought in France in 1918 with the Army. We Buxtons have a long history of serving in the Army."

"Ed told me that, Sir. Then his legacy of courage and fortitude in the face of adversity is a continuation of the legacy you helped to perpetuate. He was proud of your service in the Army." Jack ate the last bite of a donut and took a sip of his coffee. "If either of you have any questions, I'll be glad to answer them if I can. If, at a later date, you want to get in touch with me, I'll leave an address and telephone number where I can be reached. I may not be at the address when you call, but I'll get the message and will get back to you."

"You've been very kind in coming, Major. Ed wrote often of you. He liked the way you looked after the men in the company. He called you their 'Man From Maine'. He was always proud of Maine," said Mr. Buxton.

"I saw that in him. I'm glad I had a chance to meet both of you. You have my sympathy and my prayers."

"Hearing you talk about Ed the way you have, has been comforting," added Mr. Buxton, grasping his hand across the table. "He was our only child. His death has devastated us and leaves an empty space in our lives. Knowing that you was with him at the time of death has helped more than we can tell. My greatest fear was that he died alone and frightened. You've eased some of our pain. May God Bless you for that, Major."

Jack left the Buxton home feeling inadequate. If he had told them the absolute truth about the conditions they had lived and died under, it would have shattered them. "Forgive me, God, for not being more explicit."

The trip to Moosehead Lake was filled with memories of the time he and Myla had stayed there during the first week of their marriage. It was the closest thing they ever had to a honeymoon. He had booked a room at the same inn where he and Myla had stayed. It was located on a hill overlooking the lake. The minute he walked into the inn an intense sadness and an all-consuming loneliness enveloped him. He placed his overnight bag on the stand in his room and checked the view from his window. He and Myla had used a room adjacent to the one he now occupied.

The tourist season was not in full swing yet, but the hospitality industry was geared up to handle early birds. Jack was glad that the inn was relatively empty and he did not have to contend with noisy tourists. That night he ate a hearty meal in the dining room. He was restless and decided to walk down the path leading to the rocky shore of the lake. He found a convenient spot on the ledge where he sat to watch the moon shining on the water. In the distance he could hear the plaintive call of a whippoorwill. He had heard them often at his father's house. He knew what they looked like from pictures, but he never saw one in enough light to recognize it. A cool breeze blew from the west across the water. The smell of spruce and fir filled the air.

He and Myla had walked about the shore. How happy they were then! He could still hear her laugh the way she often did. Memories of those happier times were pleasant to contemplate, but they were dimmed and violated by the ugliness of the present-day reality. The more he thought of that idyllic time before the war, the sadder and angrier he became. A lump filled his throat. Memories associated with Myla brought heartache and stress to his life. With a heavy heart he headed back to the Inn where he settled in for the evening.

The next family on his list was that of Corporal Joe Planter from Bangor, a couple of hours driving time from Moosehead Lake. He called the family and set up a time, again, slightly after lunch for his visit the next day. Jack felt the tension in Mrs. Planter as he talked to her over the telephone. There was a reluctant eagerness about his proposed appointment that was evident, even over the phone. His presence forced the parents to revisit the most painful emotions a human being is capable of, and it placed a responsibility on his shoulders to deal with that pain in as gentle a manner as possible. The visits were going to be a more demanding ordeal for him than he originally thought.

That evening, Jack's thoughts turned to Lorena. He had images of her more than he had anticipated. He wasn't sure what they meant except that when he was with her he was relaxed and comfortable with who he was. Myla was increasingly making him feel incomplete and inadequate. He took a pen and paper and started a letter to Lorena:

June 1, 1945
Greenville, Maine

Dear Lorena,

A few words from the lovely Moosehead Lake. I just completed my first family visit. I was a little uncomfortable with the fact that I maintained my silence about the real severity of the prison camp. They had a right to know, but I could not bring myself to explain the squalor and bestiality of the prison experience. It would only open their emotional scars more than they already are and rub them with salt. I just could not do it. Their level of pain is already too great to describe.

I've thought often of you and the calming influence you've had on me from the first day I saw you on the hospital ship. I hope all is going well with you. The situation with my former (??) wife is very fluid. I'm still angry at what she did; yet, I can see the rationale she used in making the choice. Right now we've resolved the legal question. I'm pursuing a divorce or annulment or whatever document is needed to dissolve a promise we once made.

My dad said that a promise made is a promise kept. I've always liked the concept of simple commitment to vows. My father still thinks highly of Myla. I have not been able to shed the feelings of betrayal, so it seems that we're committed now to going our separate ways.

I almost forgot to share another piece of news with you. I'm the father of a three-and-a-half-year-old daughter named after my deceased mother, Roselyn. I haven't come to grips with that fact yet. How Roselyn will be affected by the breakup I'm not sure right now. She's an adorable child. My father worships her, and, of course, she loves her "Grandpops". I'm probably in more turmoil now than I was when I left Pearl Harbor.

There's a cool breeze sweeping across the lake, filling the air with spruce and balsam fir scents from the northern forests. A light moon is breaking through a misty overcast. I always liked the soft days and nights of June. It's a month that bridges the renewable burst of life in the springtime and the full bloom of hot summer. I wish you could be here to share it with me.

I'm not sure if what I'm feeling is friendship or something else. Perhaps I should refrain from analyzing my feelings and stop searching for a clear goal to the future. Life has suddenly become complicated. I believe I'll need more time to sort things out.

> Until next time
> All my best,
> Jack

Corporal Joseph Planter was a short, heavy-set young man of twenty years with red cheeks and a round, baby-like face. He didn't look a day over twelve years old. His perpetual smile and infectious giggle made him a favorite among his friends and buddies. He had been a squad leader in one of Jack's platoons. He did not know Planter as well as he did Ed Buxton, but Jack was present when Joe died. The seldom serious Corporal had reached the same point as many of his comrades. Life was not worth the effort any more. If there had been some sign or communication with the outside world, there would have been more encouragement and determination to cling stubbornly to life, but the outside world did not serve the prisoners well.

The night that Joe Planter died was vividly recalled by Jack. Four other inmates had died the same evening. Joe had worked in the sugar cane fields that day, eradicating weeds. He was suffering from stomach cramps and had eaten several sections of sugar cane to relieve what he thought were hunger pains. Everybody had them most of the time. On the walk back to the compound from the fields, he vomited several times, completely emptying his stomach. He had discharged large solid particles of blackened dried blood. Some who saw it remarked that he had an ulcerated stomach, a break in the lining of his stomach, and he was bleeding internally. It was a death sentence.

That night Jack sat on Planter's bamboo mat with him. One minute he was breathing and talking about his home in Bangor, and the next minute his heart stopped beating. He showed no sign of pain or discomfort; his spirit simply gave up his earthly body and ascended to a better place.

The Planter home near the outskirts of Bangor was a modest Cape Cod style home with a well-maintained lawn and gardens. Several large sugar maple trees lined the edge of the lawn, isolating the house from the street noises. A 1942 Ford sedan was parked in the driveway. Jack met Joe's mother and father and his two sisters aged ten and sixteen years. Joe was their big brother.

Jack went through the same descriptions of life in the prison camp with the Planter family as he did with the Buxtons, continuing to keep to himself the more degrading aspects of their treatment.

Mr. Planter was also a veteran of the First World War and was employed as an engineer with the Maine Highway Department. He mentioned that the agency was due for an increase in engineers because the state was building or negotiating for a heavy increase in the construction of new roads. One project that interested Jack was the proposal that was still in the conceptual stage of a new super highway from Kittery on the New Hampshire-Maine border to Portland and eventually further north into the northern reaches of the state.

Jack also gave the Planter family the medal packet and an address where he could be reached. He left the home with the same feeling of achievement and inadequacy as he had with the Buxton family. The two sisters were heavily impacted by the descriptions of the living conditions at the prison compound where their brother lived the last three years of his life. They remembered him as a young, vibrant big brother capable of overcoming anything. They had a hard time imagining that he would lie down and not want to get up again. When he left, the family was grateful for his visit, but he had reopened wounds that had partially healed, and the family was again in an emotional crisis mode. It was a trying ordeal for Jack, and he was glad to be back on the road.

The State of Maine Highway Office in Augusta was Jack's destination after leaving Bangor. He made it just before they closed for the day and was introduced to Mr. Matt Moore, the state's head engineer.

"I understand that you have several road-building proposals in the state, specifically the one from Kittery to Portland. I wanted to check on the possibilities of employment as a graduate engineer."

"You came to the right place if you're looking for a job, Major. We plan to hire several civil engineers for the work load we'll be undertaking at war's end. Have you done any design work?" asked Moore.

"Nothing on a practical basis, but it wouldn't take too long to refresh myself on essentials," claimed Jack enthusiastically.

"Well Major, since we're speculating, let me say this. Leave me your address and phone number, and I'll have a proposal for your consideration shortly. How does that sound?"

"Fair enough, Mr. Moore. I can't commit to anything right now. Your proposal will give me something specific to think about."

"I'll be in touch. Thanks for thinking about us, Major."

Jack left the office building feeling hopeful about the future. Now he had an alternative to his Army career. The proposal would help him make the decision. Driving south towards Portland, his mind was filled with possibilities for the future. Myla and his daughter continued to dominate his thoughts. How would the decision he made about a job after the war affect them? The pathos of reminiscing choked him. He looked for answers in the shadowed depths of a brilliant sun setting behind the distant White Mountains in New Hampshire. Where did he go from here?

Chapter Ten

Jack decided to drive straight to Wells that evening. About eleven o'clock he stopped in a small town north of Portland at an all-night diner for a cup of coffee and a piece of pie, if they had anything that looked appealing. That would hold him until he got to Wells. The diner was almost empty. Jack took a seat at the serving counter and gave his order to the young waitress. She brought him his coffee spilling some of it as she placed the cup and saucer in front of him. She seemed upset and apologized for the accident.

"I'm sorry, soldier."

"No problem, Ma'am. Accidents happen to everybody," Jack replied, placing a napkin in the saucer underneath the cup.

"I'll get you a fresh cup," announced the waitress, looking over his shoulder at someone in the booth behind him.

"Thank you, Miss, but you don't have to," answered Jack.

"I appreciate that," answered the waitress, serving him another cup of coffee. She then carried a hamburger to a table directly behind Jack in the corner of the diner. He heard a few mumbled words and then, a distinct thump. He turned to see what was taking place at the table. He had heard similar sounds of a blow against a human body many times in the past few years. It was accompanied by a muffled gasp for breath.

Jack left his seat. "What's going on here?" he demanded, watching the waitress hang onto the edge of the table. "Are you all right, Ma'am?"

"Yes.... Please, I don't want to be the source of trouble here," she gasped with a terrorized look in her eyes.

Two men were sitting at the booth, a teenager and an older man with broad shoulders and a beard. Without warning, the bearded man bolted from his seat, hitting Jack a heavy blow on the cheek, disappearing out the door of the diner with the younger man close behind him. The blow caught Jack off guard and knocked him against the waitress. "Let them go, Major," pleaded the waitress hysterically.

"Not for a moment, Lady," Jack cried, reaching for the door to pursue the attacker.

He saw them close the door of a Ford coupe parked beside his Nash. He rushed toward it and yanked the door handle with a powerful thrust which dragged the attacker, who was trying to hold it shut, from the seat of the Ford. He had successfully started the car, and it lurched forward, stalling against the fence surrounding the parking lot when the driver was wrenched from the seat. He was a big, heavy man. Jack released his grip in the door handle and hit the man a hard blow squarely in the face. Blood spurted from his nose. He staggered backwards against the fender of the Ford and pulled a switch blade which sparkled in the limited light of the parking lot. Jack instantly backed up and studied his opponent with calm determination.

"Put it down," Jack warned. "I'm not going to let you go, friend, knife or no knife. Any coward who hits ladies deserves a few lessons in manners."

"She's no lady, soldier boy. You should have minded your own business," threatened the attacker, wiping the blood from his upper lip.

The man was intent on using the knife. Jack saw an opening and made a feint move to the left towards his opponent as his knife arm began its deadly arc against Jack. He had expected it. In a split second Jack recoiled to the right, grasping the arm with the knife as it was stretched outward and applied all of his weight and strength into pushing the arm upward. He then leaped under the arm coming up behind the attacker, all the time holding the arm with an iron grip forcing it into the small of the attacker's back. The momentum and speed of the movement drove the attacker against the side of the Ford knocking the wind out of him.

Jack turned his assailant around and drove his knee into his groin with all the strength he could muster. The attacker dropped the knife and crumpled to the ground with a loud groan. The younger member of the pair was standing beside the Ford watching what was taking place. Jack turned to confront him. The young man quickly placed his arms in the air.

"I don't want any part of this, soldier. It's not my fight," the young man was quick to add.

"You've done what I always wanted to do with this creep," exclaimed an elderly man in a white apron standing beside Jack. "I've called the police."

"How is the waitress?" asked Jack, still breathing heavily.

"She's distraught. The police are on the way; they'll drop her off at the doctor she uses. Her husband was recently killed in action on Okinawa. Poor Marie. Her husband was home for a week three months ago. Last month she received word of his death. The slimeball you tangled with is her brother-in-law. He was always after her. She was petrified of him and had to fight him off several times. I'd be obliged if you would join me in pressing charges against him, Major."

"It'll be a pleasure, Sir," responded Jack, buttoning his jacket.

The attacker slowly pulled himself up against the Ford. Dark piercing eyes filled with rage and hatred glared at Jack as he stepped in front of the man and delivered another powerful knee to his groin. A deep groan again emanated from the large hulk as he slid spread-eagle fashion to the ground. Jack kicked the attacker in the groin with his foot for good measure. A howl of pain filled the night air. "That's for not apologizing to the lady and for being so unfriendly towards me. Try it again, and I'll really hurt you, buddy."

"My God, don't kill him," cried the diner owner as a police car turned into the lot with blue lights blinking. The owner described what happened to the policeman whom he knew personally and made an official charge against the attacker. The policeman carefully recorded what he was told and asked Jack for a statement. Five minutes later, Jack signed the written statement and helped the officer place the prisoner in the police car.

"We've had a lot of trouble with this character," said the policeman. "He's hurt a lot of people in the area. You did a complete job on him, Major. Congratulations, he got what was coming to him at last. Usually he walks away unscathed with everybody too scared to make a charge stick."

"I was probably a little extreme, but I agree he asked for what he got. Are you going to take the young lady home, officer?" asked Jack.

"I'd be glad to, but she wanted to finish her shift. She's had a rough time of it with her husband being killed. I know her family," said the officer. "Thanks for the help, Major. If you hadn't been in the diner, the owner would have tackled our prisoner and most likely have been hurt. I was a sergeant in the last war. They wouldn't take me when Pearl Harbor was bombed, so I took the police job here in town. Good luck to you, Sir."

"You're welcome, officer. It looks as if the town is well-served. I'm going back in to have a cup of coffee and a piece of custard pie."

"Best pies in the state," replied the policeman, getting into his car.

Jack took his seat at the counter. Marie, the waitress, was still distraught and nervous. "How are you feeling, young lady?"

"I'm so sorry that I was the cause of all the fuss," she exclaimed. "He hit me on my neck and shoulder. I was afraid for my baby. I hope he did not hurt you." She looked closely at the red mark on his cheek.

"In all of the scuffle I forgot about that. I'm fine. The police officer told me that you wanted to finish your shift. Is there anything I can do to help?"

"I'll be all right, Major," answered the young waitress, placing a fresh cup of coffee and a large piece of pie in front of him. "You remind me of my husband. He had the same kind of eyes as you when he said good-bye to me for the last time. Thank you for doing what you did. I really appreciate it."

"Young lady, you can reward me by taking the time to see that the coward in the police car is sentenced for a long time. Promise me that you'll take the time to see that justice for you, your unborn child, and your deceased husband is done. Also, keep alive the memory of your husband to your child so that he or she can appreciate the legacy of courage and commitment that he left behind. Protecting those who cannot protect themselves is a noble endeavor and is its own reward."

They talked about small town affairs, the local ball team and the war in general. Jack finished the pie and coffee and was prepared to leave when the owner poked his head through the window leading to the small kitchen to announce: "It's on the house, Major. Any time you're passing through, please stop in and let us treat you. That will be our pleasure."

"Thanks, Sir. The policeman was right, the best pie in the state!" replied Jack truthfully. He swung off the stool and confronted the waitress. "You take good care of yourself and that precious life you and your husband created. Good-bye."

"Good-bye, Major," she said, kissing him on the cheek. "Good luck to you wherever you're going."

The young, courageous widow made him think of what Myla must have been going through when she first heard of his demise. He left the diner in a pensive mood.

The two-day trip had been an eventful period for Jack. By the time he pulled into his father's driveway, he was tired. The house was dark. Jack mused that his dad still turned in early and got up early. He let himself in and went directly to bed. He woke up the next morning with a surprise. Roselyn had quietly tiptoed into his room to tickle his nose with a chicken feather.

"What?" exclaimed Jack, startled by the prank. He woke from a sound sleep. Roselyn and his father standing in the door were laughing at him. "Dad, you're showing her some bad habits," scolded Jack, pleased to see his daughter laugh at the trick. She threw her head back and laughed like her mother.

"Coffee is on," announced his father. "C'mon, Rose. We can start on our cereal while your daddy gets dressed. I've got something to discuss with you when you come down, Son."

Twenty minutes later, Jack presented himself at the kitchen table, showered and shaved. The right side of his face slightly swollen. His father was quick to notice it.

"What's the other fellow look like, Jack?"

"Would you believe that he's in a lot worse shape," he joked. "A low-life character attacked a waitress at a diner. I stopped him, that's all. Well, good morning, Roselyn. It's a surprise to see you here this morning."

"Mommy said I could stay until she comes to get me. Grandpops and I ate lobsters last night," she said between spoons full of Rice Krispies cereal.

"Did you save any lobsters for Daddy?"

"No. Grandpops says that they're best eaten fresh."

"Grandpops is correct. What did you want to talk to me about, Dad?"

"There were two calls for you while you were gone. One from a Colonel Adams at Fort Belvoir wanted to know if you could cut your leave short to take a position on a Veterans board being set up to aid the veterans who have been injured physically or emotionally. It's a system to help them make the transition from military to civilian life. The second call was from a Lieutenant Jerome Wilkins in Albany, New York. He sounded upset and confused. He said he knew you. I have the telephone numbers for both of the men."

Jack had never heard of Colonel Adams. "I know Lieutenant Wilkins. He was in the prison compound with me. Did he mention any kind of trouble he might be in?" asked Jack, wondering what the call could mean.

"Here comes Mommy," shouted Roselyn, looking out the window as her mother drove into the driveway.

Myla walked into the room, acknowledged Jack and his father and took a seat beside Roselyn. "I didn't mean to intrude," she apologized, taking a closer look at Jack. "What happened to you?"

"I had a difference of opinion with a rabble-rouser last night. He looks worse than I do."

"Pops told me that you'd be gone for a while visiting families of men who died in prison camp. It must have been horrible for all of you."

"It wasn't easy," answered Jack, not wanting to get into that discussion with her.

"How did you get the necessary gasoline to make the trip? The gas coupons I left in the car were only good for a few gallons per week," asked Myla, wiping Roselyn's mouth clean.

"I was issued a VIP card for gasoline purchases when I was given my furlough papers. I probably could have purchased most any amount I wanted without it, as long as I was in uniform," Jack replied, recalling how most men and women in uniform were met with respect and admiration and frequently were extended favors. It was a common practice all over the country during the war years.

"You're probably right," mused Myla, avoiding his glances. "I came to get Roselyn. Mother will look after her today while I'm in school."

"What's Jeff doing for work? I haven't seen him around since I came back," Jack wondered aloud.

"He's working at the Portsmouth Naval Yard on a night shift."

"I see...," said Jack, interrupted by the telephone ringing.

Pops Ross answered it. "Hello. Yes, Major Ross is here. Just a moment please," he said passing the receiver to Jack. "It's Lieutenant Wilkins."

"Hi, Jerome. How are you enjoying your furlough?"

"Nothing has gone right, Major," answered Lieutenant Wilkins. "I would never have bothered you on leave except that one of our men from Bataan, Sergeant Dave McCoy, is in prison at Albany. He went berserk and cleaned out a barroom in the city. Without going into detail, he returned home to learn that his fiancée had married someone else."

"I can appreciate his feelings, Jerome. God, I haven't been able to get my own life in order, I'm not sure I could help much. What did you have in mind?" Jack asked.

"If both of us appear at his hearing, maybe the judge will consider what he's been through and go easy on him. He was my platoon sergeant, and I relied on him a lot. He's a good soldier, and I still feel responsible for him."

Jack thought about the situation. Lieutenant Jerome Wilkins was a unique soldier. He had graduated from West Point in 1941 and was shipped immediately after graduation to the Philippine Islands. The men in his platoon loved him because they knew that he always had their welfare in mind. He was born to be a soldier and had the knack of carrying authority and responsibility of command without arrogance or posturing. He was the last platoon leader on Bataan to stop firing at the enemy when they were ordered to surrender.

"I've visited only two of the seven families in my area, Jerome," answered Jack. "Give me a time and place and I'll be there."

"Thanks, Major. I knew I could count on you. His hearing is coming up at 10:00 AM at the Albany District Court House day after tomorrow. I'll meet you at the Court House prior to the hearing. Thanks again, Sir. If nothing else transpires from our appearance, it will send Sergeant McCoy a message that he's not alone out there in the world."

"How lucky first platoon was to draw you as a commander, Jerome. You're like a mother hen to the men. I always admired how you cared for them. How are things going for you?"

"I'm being treated like royalty, Major. I did not make any commitments before I left for the Philippines, so I wasn't disappointed when I returned to see how things had changed. My home phone is Albany 377J if you need to contact me. Thanks for offering to help. The gasoline cards we were issued are a big help, aren't they?"

"I'll say they are. I didn't realize how difficult it was for the civilian population to get around. I'll see you day after tomorrow at the Albany Court House."

Myla had been watching Jack closely, listening to his conversation. She understood how shattering the situation he found at home must have been for him. One thing that had not changed was the way Jack handled responsibilities. Caring for the men in his command was always something he took seriously. His response to a request for help was in keeping with his character, and she was pleased to see that that part of Jack remained the same.

"Well, Pops, I must be going. Thanks for looking after Roselyn. Come on, Honey. Mommy has got to get to school."

Roselyn approached Grandpops and Jack with open arms and kissed both of them on the cheek. "Good-bye, Daddy, and you, too, Grandpops."

"Bye, little lady," said Jack, touched by her innocence. He turned to look at Myla. "It was nice of you to make the Nash available to me. I hate to put more miles on it, but there are some things that need to be done."

"I couldn't agree more, Jack. Have a good trip." Myla helped Roselyn put on a light sweater folded on the kitchen counter. When she reached for it she noticed a letter on the counter addressed to Jack from an Ensign Lorena Kelly.

After Myla left, Jack sat back down at the table. His father gave him the letter.

"This came for you yesterday," said his father with raised eyebrows.

"Oh, it's from a nurse I had in Pearl Harbor," answered Jack without further explanation.

Pearl Harbor
June 5, 1945

Dear Jack,

A quick note to let you know that I've been given an extended furlough, the first I've had since I joined the Navy in 1941. I'm leaving Pearl Harbor tomorrow and hope to be home in Warrensburg as soon as wings can carry me there. I need this opportunity to resolve a number of issues in my life. I've been running away from them for too long. I'm seeking solace and solitude to get better acquainted with the person that I am and to formulate some kind of goal for the future.

If you write to me, my new address is Route Nine Warrensburg, New York. My phone number is 92W.

I hope that you are settling into normal routines that are meaningful to you.

All my best,
Lorena

Chapter Eleven

The drive to Albany was uneventful. The trip gave Jack an opportunity to reflect on everything taking place in his life. It seemed so complicated, when all he wanted was simplicity. He needed direction and motivation that would give him some assurance that he was correctly handling the opportunity to make decisions for himself after three and a half years. Right now, he didn't rate himself very high in that department.

The radio stations through New Hampshire and Vermont were filled with songs popular with the members of the armed services and their families left at home. Enduring hope and love in the face of adversity and austerity were common subjects of the songs. Love and acknowledgment of promises made were themes played over and over regardless of the name of the song or the singer. "*I'll Walk Alone*," by Dinah Shore; "*When the Lights Go On Again, All Over The World*," by Vaughn Monroe; and "*I'll Be Seeing You In All The Old Familiar Places*," by Vera Lynn, made him feel more alone than ever.

Jack had been out of the picture for so long that even though he was a free man, he had not yet caught up with the pace of things around him. Most of the popular songs were unfamiliar. His recovery period after being rescued from certain death took place within a cocoon filled with support systems of every dimension one could ask for. He went from an atmosphere of total submission to the authoritative rules and regulations of the hospital and therapy center where compliance was up to the individual. At times the freedom to make decisions was frightening to him.

The prospect of a divorce also weighed heavily on Jack's mind. He had flaunted it in front of Myla because he wanted to show her that he was still in command of decisions about his life. It was as much a request for debate as it was a statement of policy. It was an ad hoc explanation that he had hoped would shock her into indignation, even anger, that he should entertain such a preposterous thing. Instead, she calmly accepted his proposal without protest or further discussion. Her lack of dissent was significant, and, to him, it indicated that whatever they once had was gone forever. It was unsettling and had kept him in a nervous state of anxiety ever since.

Before Jack left Wells for New York State, he had spoken to a lawyer friend of the family to start divorce proceedings. After the visit, he was physically sick to his stomach. He hated Myla for forcing the move upon him. Didn't she know that he was not capable of making long range decisions so early in his recovery? He thought a lot about it on his trip to Albany and questioned if it was the best solution for all concerned. He wasn't sure, especially when an image of Roselyn reaching out to hug him tweaked his heartstrings. There were no simple answers, only complications without ready solutions.

Roselyn was the one to be the most hurt, no matter what happened. The past few days that he had a chance to be around her, she had filled his heart with joy. She made him feel needed. His desire and responsibility to be a part of her life was the only portion of his life that was firmly anchored in reality.

Jack arrived in Albany after dark and found a vacancy in a hotel near the Court House. The first thing he did was place a call to Jerome to announce his arrival. Afterwards he stretched out on the bed, clasped his hands behind his head and thought about the letter he received from Lorena. She was within sixty miles from Albany.

He leaped from the bed and took a chance that she might be at the number she had given him. His palms were moist and cold as he lifted the phone and gave the number to the operator. It rang three times. He was ready to hang up when a voice he would recognize anywhere came on the line.

"Hello."

"Hi, Lorena. This is Jack Ross. I took a chance you might be home. It's nice to speak to you again."

"This is a surprise, Jack. I got in yesterday. Yours is the first call on the phone since I requested a reconnection," she told him.

Jack detected a weariness and a somber tone in her voice. "Is this a bad time for me to call?"

"No," she replied. "I'm just exhausted from the trip. I needed to get away from the wards at the hospital. It was beginning to overwhelm me. My commanding officer ordered me on leave. I didn't object, but that's enough of my troubles. How have things been going for you?"

He told her about his visit to Albany and the court hearing in the morning. He also explained that he was seeking a divorce from Myla and that he had a daughter, Roselyn.

"Oh my," she sighed approvingly. "A little girl may just be what her daddy needs right now. Congratulations, Jack."

"It hasn't sunk in completely, Lorena," he admitted. Talking with her gave him that same feeling of completeness he experienced the first time he noticed her in the ward on the hospital ship. Chaos and turmoil disappeared, and a wonderful feeling that everything was going to work out for the best filled his heart. She was a lifeline of hope and faith for the future. Serenity emanated from her even over the phone. It made him want to be with her.

"When I'm finished here in Albany, I could swing north to Warrensburg if you don't mind."

She hesitated for a moment. "I'm very unsettled, Jack, but it'll be nice to see you again. Please call before you come."

"That's a promise. I'll see you soon."

"Good luck at court. The soldier was fortunate to have you as a commander. Good night, Jack."

The next morning, Jack met Lieutenant Wilkins at the District Court. The trim young West Point graduate filled him in on the charges against Platoon Sergeant Dave McCoy.

"McCoy singularly took on a barroom filled with civilians and did a lot of damage. He was drunk out of his noggin," related Wilkins. "I was surprised because he had a reputation of being a moderate drinker."

"It doesn't take much to push a man over the edge," replied Jack, thinking of his own actions at the diner. "Is McCoy married or engaged?"

"That's the fly in the ointment, Major. He was engaged to a girl before he was shipped out to the Philippines in 1941. When he returned home, the fiancée was married to someone else and had a baby boy. You know the story better than anyone. It was more than he could handle. He told me that his fiancée wants to have the marriage annulled or dissolved and that she is willing to marry him, but her husband is the father of the child and refuses to do that. It's a mess."

A security guard unlocked the court house door, beckoning them into the courtroom. A police officer escorted Sergeant McCoy to the defendant's table where Jack and Jerome were sitting. McCoy was a short, muscular man with wide shoulders. His sandy brown hair was neatly trimmed and combed. His uniform fit him as if he was poured into it. He carried himself with confidence. His lip was swollen, and he had a red bruise over his left eye. When he saw the two officers at the table, he acknowledged them with a sheepish smile, and a look of shame came over his face. He found it difficult to make eye contact with them. He was a powerful young man and moved with ease.

"I'm sorry for causing so much trouble, Lieutenant Wilkins. It's nice to see you again, Major Ross. Thanks for coming. I really appreciate it," said Sergeant McCoy.

The clerk of court read the charges against the sergeant. They included assault and battery against an undisclosed number of people in the nightclub, disturbing the peace, and destruction of furniture and fixtures in the lounge area. There was another charge unrelated to the barroom incident that Lieutenant Wilkins was unaware of. It said that the Sergeant had violated a court order to stay away from a certain residence in Albany. Jack studied the sergeant while the charges were being read. He stood proud and erect, looking squarely at the clerk of court.

"You've heard the charges, Sergeant McCoy," stated the Judge in a slow precise voice. "How do you wish to plead?"

"I plead guilty to the charges in the barroom, Your Honor. This is the first time I learned of anything like a restraining order at the house where my former fiancée was living," Sergeant McCoy stated firmly.

"I notice two Army officers at the table with you, Sergeant. Do they wish to address the court?"

Jack and Jerome nodded their heads in the affirmative.

"Go ahead, Major," whispered Lieutenant Wilkins.

"Thank you, Your Honor," said Jack. "I'm Major Jack Ross. I was Sergeant McCoy's company commander on Bataan. Lieutenant Wilkins, here with me, was his platoon leader. The three of us were imprisoned in a Japanese prison camp on Luzon for three and a half years and just returned to the United States days ago. I appreciate the opportunity to address the court. It's important for the court to understand where the sergeant has been and the kind of conditions he had to endure during his confinement without any word from or to the outside world for that long period of suffering and deprivation.

"Sergeant McCoy and thousands of young men left home filled with a concept of duty that was synonymous with defending liberty and a way of life we all treasure. They believed that their sacrifice was worth the alternative, slavery at the hands of brutal dictators. When duty whispered, thou must, American youth replied, I can, and went into battle fortified by the fervor of their convictions that God was on their side.

"Those young men who rode jauntily off to war returned as men, old before their years. Many had deep and lasting psychic wounds that will always be with them. The prison camp where Sergeant McCoy lived those long years are beyond description. Filth, degradation, starvation, death, and the loss of pride readily come to my mind. Men laid down at night and willed themselves to die because living had simply become too much effort. Those who died were envied, for they were no longer suffering. We had to bury our friends and companions when we had little strength to dig their graves. Opposition to the guards was impossible. It only brought on additional brutal treatment and broken bodies.

"Those of us who survived the ordeal did so because we had found strength and refuge in dreams of home and the better times recalled in our lives. I want to impress upon the court the significance of those dreams. They took on a dimension far more important than baseless fantasies. Without that element of normal life to cling to, a lot more men would have been buried in unmarked graves in the jungles of Luzon. Adjustment from the incarceration period to freedom of choices was not easy once we were rescued. Things changed and people changed, yet the freed prisoners still clung to a period in their lives which maintained their sanity in the face of abject adversity. Ultimately they had to face reality like Sergeant McCoy. Things had changed. The dreams that had become so crucial, to him and others like him, turned out to be a deception, a cruel quirk of fate. Reality did not measure up to those dreams. It would shatter most strong normal people. To those who were emotionally fragile, reality became intolerable.

"Lieutenant Wilkins and I are not here to condone Sergeant McCoy's transgressions. He readily admits them. I want to bring to the court's attention that he wears the Combat Infantryman's Badge and a Purple Heart. Few people in this room will ever be asked to do what it took to earn those two decorations. I want the court to understand what this man has been through. Lieutenant Wilkins and I have come here in defense of a fine soldier, and we ask the court to be lenient. Thank you."

"How far did you travel to be here this morning, Major Ross?" asked the Judge.

"About a hundred and twenty-five miles from Wells, Maine, Your Honor," answered Jack.

"I see. Thank you for your efforts, Major. Do you have anything to add, Lieutenant Wilkins?"

"I do, Your Honor," added Lieutenant Wilkins. He corroborated what Jack had said and went into the more personal aspect of Sergeant McCoy's trauma of finding that his fiancée was married to another man and had a child with him. The betrayal of trust was difficult to handle.

After Lieutenant Wilkins's dissertation, the Judge asked the Sergeant if he had anything to say. The sturdy soldier stood up straight and answered: "I'm ashamed and embarrassed with my conduct since I returned to Albany, Your Honor. I had been looking forward to coming home and getting married to the girl I left behind. When I got here I found that she was already married to another person and was pregnant. For days, I didn't know what I was going to do. My world had collapsed, and I was unprepared for the real world. All during my time at the prison camp, thoughts of what was waiting for me here is all that kept me alive. I didn't care what happened to me at that point.

"When I walked into the court room this morning I was pleased to see that my old company and platoon commanders had come to help me out. I'll pay for the damages to the barroom. Sitting here listening to the Major and the Lieutenant take time to speak on my behalf, I've decided that there's nothing here in Albany for me anymore. The Army is my only home for now. If you'll give me the opportunity to return to my Army duty station, I promise to do so."

The Judge was impressed with the sincerity of the Sergeant's declaration. "It's not the intention of this Court to place unnecessary burdens on those who have been in combat defending our nation. In light of the prestigious efforts of Major Ross and Lieutenant Wilkins and your admission of responsibility, I'll dismiss the charges against you. Thank you, gentlemen. Next on the agenda!"

Jack left Albany by mid-afternoon feeling good that he could help out a fellow soldier. The brotherhood of combatants was a strong bond that sustained many in times of need. Perhaps Sergeant McCoy displayed more courage when faced with the reality of his personal situation than he did in the stinking jungles of the Philippines. Jack and

Jerome were pleased with his decision to step off in another direction. It sounded easy, but Jack knew how difficult it really was and how tragic the decision was to make for such a proud man as Sergeant McCoy. They all had a steak dinner at a fine restaurant, said good-bye, and went their separate ways. If they remained in the Army long enough, the chances were good that their paths would cross again.

Jack took a hotel room on the waterfront of Lake George and immediately called a Colonel Adams at Fort Belvoir. The colonel had called to offer him a position as part of a headquarters company concerned with assisting war veterans make the transition to civilian life. It was being administered under the auspices of the Veteran's Administration. Primarily, the job of the newly formed group was to administer the far-reaching and generous Serviceman's Readjustment Act of 1944. It soon became known as the GI Bill of Rights and provided low-interest loans for mortgages and living expenses for those who wanted to attend colleges or trade schools. It also provided financial assistance for veterans who could not immediately find meaningful employment.

Jack was impressed with the benefit package being made available to veterans and gladly accepted the duty station. It did not curtail any of his furlough which would end September 1st, but it did give an element of stability to his plans for the future. He had hoped for the command of an infantry company, but the new billet sounded challenging. At least he knew what was expected of him once he reported for duty. At that time he could evaluate his military and civilian options.

Checking his note pad for Lorena's telephone number, Jack called her. The phone rang several times before a voice answered.

"Hello."

"Hello, is that you, Lorena?" afraid that something had happened to her.

"Yes, it's me," she answered in a tremulous voice.

"I'm sorry if this is a bad time for me to call?"

"I suppose it is," she admitted in a low voice. "It has been difficult."

"Can a friend help, or do you prefer to be alone?"

"I don't know, Jack. I didn't realize it was going to hurt so much. If you want, you can stop by. I won't be very good company...."

"Dear lady, for once in your life stop thinking of everybody else and be a little selfish. Everybody needs a helping hand at some time or another. You were there for me and hundreds of others when we needed it. I'd consider it a privilege to be there for you. Otherwise what are friends for?"

"Thank you for that."

"I have the directions you gave me last night. I'll be there as soon as I can."

Chapter Twelve

The small two-story house was located on a ledge outcrop above a small stream with a range of blue-tinted mountains in the background. The minute Jack turned off the main road he was struck by the beauty of the setting with large towering white pine trees lining the driveway. The house was painted white with red shutters. It had a porch, on the side near the drive, that continuing around to the rear of the house and blended into a flat section of ledge next to the river.

A feeling of peace came over him as he stepped out of the Nash. The house nestled within the pine trees cultivated an image of harmony. It was an extension of the serenity and calm she projected. A soft breeze made a hushed whirring sound as it flowed through the tree canopies high above his head. He felt the peace, but there was something else that radiated from the site, the sadness of Lorena's loss.

It was easy for Jack to understand how happy Lorena and her husband must have been in such a warm, graceful setting. Feeling like an intruder, he walked from the drive to the ledge at the back of the house. The riverbed narrowed below the house and was running high from recent rains. The foaming water threw itself against the rocky channel with a soft gurgling sound that was soothing to the ear. He knocked on the door. A voice within called to him.

"Come in, Jack."

He entered a sitting room decorated with knotty pine paneling covering the walls and a large stone-faced fireplace on the opposite wall from the French doors that opened onto the deck and ledge. The room carried that same warm inviting sensation that filled his senses.

111

"I came as soon as I could," Jack said, noticing Lorena with a bathrobe around her, sitting on a couch beside the fireplace in the center of the room. "I hope I'm not intruding."

"Hello, Jack," she said, rising to greet him. Her eyes were red and swollen. "Please excuse me. I'm ill-prepared to play the congenial host right now."

Jack saw the pain and trauma in her face. For a long time she had put her feelings to one side while she attended to the needs of the sick and injured. Her return to the scene of happier days with her dead husband, Robert, had been more difficult than she expected. Her grief could no longer be denied.

"It's nice to see you again, Lorena."

"The minute I came through the door Bob's presence in the house became overwhelming," Lorena continued. "I see and feel him everywhere. It's almost as if I was learning of his death for the first time. We were so happy here in our little house."

"Happiness and harmony radiate from this place. Now that I've seen it, I understand how much it meant to the two of you. What a wonderful retreat from the rest of the world. I never knew your husband, but this home you shared with him tells me a lot about him. His gentle ways and patience are still in this room. I can feel it, too," said Jack, putting his arms around her.

"He was a high school teacher, and the students loved him. I didn't think it would affect me like it has. He's been gone for two years; yet, I can picture him standing out there on the ledge watching a sunset in the mountains to the west. He found them inspiring and often called me to his side to enjoy it with him. He was a strong, gentle man…"

"The two of you were blessed with something special. Some couples never reach that level of intimacy. At least your memories, echoes of the past as you call them, are pleasant ones. I'm not sure if it's possible for a person to love too much. Letting go can be difficult, maybe even impossible. The memories can be precious, deep and long-lasting." Jack's personal feelings were not too far removed from the ones Lorena was preoccupied with. The only exception was that he lost Myla to another man. The loss was not as permanent, but the rejection stung with a viciousness he still could not accept.

Jack continued, "I listen to myself in disbelief. I haven't been able to confront my own situation with a rational mind. Who am I to offer platitudes or comfort? What I'm trying to say, Lorena, is that it's important to me to see you happy and content with your life."

"I believe you and appreciate your concern," Lorena replied.

"You've become a benchmark of sorts whereby I can measure how well I'm handling transition from the prison environment to the complexities of human relationships in a world at war."

"And what do you think that signifies, Jack?" she asked with interest.

"Don't you know, Lorena?" asked Jack, wondering if he had made a mistake coming to her house.

"No, I don't know, Jack, and I'm too confused and weary right now to try and figure it out."

"I believe I've fallen in love with you in spite of the fact that neither of us are prepared for deep relationships. My acknowledgment of the feelings has left me in more chaos than ever. It has fed the fires of uncertainty and indecision. Nothing seems permanent or predictable in this crazy world, except for the gift you have of bringing order to chaos. You have that wonderful capacity to make people feel empowered and comfortable with themselves."

"Don't you think that you're having a classic case of transference, Jack?" she replied pointedly.

"I've thought about that, too," he admitted, wishing that he had not bared his soul to her at this vulnerable time. She had enough on her mind without adding more stress to her life. "You know, Lorena, I came here to see you because I thought a friend might want a friend to lean on. I'm sorry. I'm thinking only of myself, and that's being selfish. I care enough for you to want your well-being."

"This is becoming a very heavy conversation, Jack."

"I apologize, Lorena. Have you eaten dinner yet?"

"No, I haven't been hungry lately."

"Would you like to go out somewhere, maybe at Lake George or some other place for a quiet dinner?" asked Jack, feeling helpless she was so distraught.

"That sounds like a good idea. Would you excuse me for a few minutes while I freshen up and change?"

"Please, take all the time you need."

Twenty minutes later Lorena presented herself to him in a green print dress with lace trim around her neck. It was the first time Jack had seen her dressed in something besides her nurse uniform. She was beautiful with her natural blonde hair pulled up to the top of her head, making her look taller.

"You're lovely, Lorena."

"Thank you, Jack. I bought the dress in Pearl Harbor two years ago and have never worn it until now."

He escorted her to the Nash holding the door open for her to get in. They drove to a small inn on the western shore of Lake George. The inn and restaurant were a classic example of Victorian elegance. They dined on a terrace overlooking the water. It was dark by the time they got seated. The lights from homes and cottages along the shoreline illuminated the gentle wash of the waves upon the rocks. Jack was surprised at the lights at night. He told her about the blackout that still existed along the coastal regions of Wells even though the war with Germany was over.

"How did your court appearance turn out?" asked Lorena.

"Better than we expected. Sergeant McCoy was released on probation from all charges. I expect that right now he's on his way back to his next duty station. He may make a career out of the Army. I guess he turned a barroom upside down before three police officers were able to subdue him," grinned Jack.

"It was nice of you and Lieutenant Wilkins to be there for him. I admire that kind of loyalty. I've seen a lot of it among the soldiers and sailors. It's too bad that more of that kind of commitment isn't shown in civilian life," mused Lorena.

"Civilian life lacks the shared danger and trauma of combat. The battlefield is a brutal killing field yet; it's a great equalizer that instantly bonds strangers together into a brotherhood of warriors for a lifetime. It's hard to explain, but civilian life does not present such demanding decisions for most humans, and that is probably as it should be."

"I've experienced that fellowship in the wards. It's a noble and healing relationship."

"I'm glad that you have some time off," said Jack, raising his glass of wine toward her. "I propose a toast to a brave lady who has suffered greatly and continues to give her all to those in need of her care. I salute you, Ensign Kelly."

She raised her glass with misty eyes and smiled at him. The dim lights of the terrace showered down upon her, creating soft shadows across her face. She was a vision of loveliness. How her husband must have loved her, Jack thought, watching her fight to control the tears. Her moist eyes reflected the fatigue and sorrow she held inside. He admired the courage she had to control disastrous events in her life with grace and dignity. There was a faraway look in her soft green eyes. She was with him at the table, but a part of her was somewhere else – echoes of the past, again. He understood.

After they had completed their meals, Jack drove around the lake. It was a refreshingly warm night in June. The sky was filled with stars sparkling from the dark voids. Here in the heart of the country it was hard to imagine that a war was still raging across the Pacific and men were still dying. They didn't talk much after leaving the inn. Something was happening that neither of them talked about. Jack turned the Nash into a scenic pullout on the lake and stopped. A half moon had climbed high into the sky. Its beam of light created black shadows beneath the towering white pine trees lining the shore of the lake. The distinctive smell of sweet fern filled the air.

Moonbeams of light cut through the front seat of the Nash landing on Lorena, highlighting her delicate facial features. She sat beside Jack watching the water with her chin held high. A lone tear formed in her left eye and rolled down her cheek. Jack placed his arm around her and watched the tear. He kissed it away.

"If I had the power, I'd wipe out all of the sorrow you're carrying," he whispered in her ear.

"You're a good man, Jack. It's a beautiful night. Beauty makes me cry. It has been nice being with you and sharing some of our feelings. A friend is always comforting…"

"Will you stay with me tonight, Lorena?" he asked, surprised at his boldness. He had listened to his heart and could not deny what he felt when she was with him.

"Do you know what you're asking, Jack?" she questioned, looking into his eyes.

"I admit it's sudden and bold and probably inappropriate at this stage of our relationship; yet, it feels right," Jack explained. "I believe that I'm falling in love with you, Lorena." He held her close and kissed her forehead.

"I'm not sure that this is something we should do, Jack."

"If you're uncertain, I understand. More than anything else I want you to be happy, and I want to be worthy of your respect. I haven't felt right about myself or anything else since I left you at Pearl Harbor. The minute I spoke to you over the phone and saw you at your home, everything seemed more in order. It's hard for me to explain because it's so elusive. It was in that spirit that I asked you. I want to be with you, and I feel good when I am. Maybe you can figure it out, Lenora. The only thing wrong with that picture is that it's inherently selfish."

"You're not selfish, Jack," she cried, lifting her lips to his. "I'll stay with you tonight. I don't want to be alone either."

Later that evening at the hotel, Jack and Lorena engaged in an intense act of love and became as one. Two confused and lonely people found release and solace in each other's arms. For a short span of time the world and its infinite capacity to hurt was forgotten, and the desire to love and be loved ruled their small world.

The next morning Lorena woke up in the hotel bedroom. The sun was shining through the open windows announcing the birth of a new day. She reached out for Jack beside her – he was not there! She sat upright wondering if he had gone to the bathroom. His uniform was still draped over the valet where he had placed it last night. Suddenly she heard a guttural sound on the opposite side of the bed. She leaned over and saw Jack coiled in a fetal position lying on the carpeted floor.

He appeared to be sleeping, but sweat was running down his face and his arms were crossed above his head as if he was protecting it from some type of blows. Lorena called to him in a loud voice. He did not respond. She leaped from bed and sat beside him, gently placing his head in her lap. She tried to console him.

"It's over now, Jack," she repeated over and over, wiping the perspiration from his face. She checked for a pulse. His heart was beating rapidly. Lorena wrapped her arms around his tense body. He was reliving an experience from the prison camp. Chances were that he would never be free of the horror unless someone filled his heart so full of love that there was no more room for anything else. Displacing horrific memories would be a measure of true love. Suddenly the tension in his body lessened and Jack opened his eyes. He stared into Lorena's face and smiled. "What a wonderful way to wake up in the morning," he said in a strained voice.

"You frightened me, Jack. Why did you sleep on the floor?" she asked.

"I don't know, Lorena. It doesn't happen every night. Sometimes I find myself on the floor in the morning. I know it sounds ridiculous, but I can't explain why I would give up a perfectly comfortable bed for a hard floor."

"It's not ridiculous when you think where you've been. Sleeping on the ground was a natural nightly phenomenon, a conditioned reflex for over three years. It'll take time to work that out of your system. The memories of that place are another matter. Hopefully they'll be displaced when you get your life in order and find happiness and fulfillment."

He listened to the sound of her calm voice and felt her arms around him. A feeling of humility and a sense of privilege enveloped him. Lorena had that magic ability to wipe out ugly thoughts and replace them with feelings of well-being. She cultivated hope and a sense of purpose without realizing she was doing it.

"Come, you'll catch a chill here on the floor," she said, wiping the sweat from his brow.

"I'll jump in the shower," he replied, putting his arms around her. "How nice it is to be with you like this. Any regrets?"

"No regrets, Jack," she responded. "It was a beautiful evening. I'll shower after you and then we'll have breakfast."

"I was going to suggest that."

An hour later, they ordered bacon and eggs and plenty of coffee in the hotel dining room. Lorena had combed her hair so that it fell loose about her shoulders. No matter how she wore it she was attractive. She had a regal air of confidence and control. Yesterday Jack had caught a glimpse of the depth of her grief for her dead husband, and he searched for some way to help her. There was an elusive mystique about her that defied definition. He had seen that very private side of her from the beginning. It was an integral part of her allure, and his fascination for her had deepened steadily.

"I haven't heard you talk about your daughter, Jack. Four-year-old children are at a precious stage in their lives. How do you feel being a daddy?" asked Lorena, watching him closely for his response.

"My daughter is a beautiful little girl," said Jack pensively. "You know, Lorena, I'm angry at myself. When I first heard about her I didn't know how to handle it. The first time I met her at my father's place it was as if I was a stranger. I certainly didn't feel like a father. She has acknowledged me as her daddy, and I'm thrilled when she puts her little arms around me, but it's still something I have not become accustomed to. I'm closer to her now than that first day, but I feel that it should be deeper and more meaningful than it is. She deserves more from me, and I'm still like a stranger."

"When all is said and done, Jack, you are a stranger. If you harbor regrets or anger at Myla then your acceptance of her may be inhibited by that anger," suggested Lorena. "Your perception of Myla will be apparent to your daughter."

"I guess I've just got to be more patient. Roselyn is named after my mother who died when I was born. I've already started divorce proceedings. Roselyn becomes a complication in any settlement. I've always wondered what it would be like to have children," said Jack.

"Jack," scolded Lorena. "Little Roselyn has to be more than a complication."

"I didn't mean it that way. I'm concerned that whatever takes place she'll end up getting hurt which isn't fair. She's blameless in this whole affair."

"Give it some time, Jack. Things on the home front are not as you hoped they would be; it could be worse. Imagine how you would feel if she was not your child?" asked Lorena. "When we've finished breakfast do you want to come to my house?"

"I'll take you home if that's what you want. I can appreciate how you feel about your place. I don't want to violate the memories that you have there. When a house becomes a home it also becomes a sanctuary for body and soul. Right now, it probably takes on an added significance because your husband is gone, and he left you with memories that will take a long time for you to reconcile before you're able to let go of that period in your life. Memories exist in every corner where you dreamed of the future and plotted its course. If you don't mind, I'll drop you off and head back to New Hampshire and Massachusetts for more family visits."

"You speak about homes from experience. Is that what you felt about your ocean cottage?" asked Lorena perceptively.

"Yes, you could say that," replied Jack. "What I'm trying to say is that I don't want to violate your space of very private and intimate memories. Later, when you've worked things out so that you're more comfortable about the past, it'll be easier and more appropriate. Private sanctuaries should remain that way for as long as you wish."

"Do you feel that way about your cottage?"

"Yes, I believe so," answered Jack, perceiving the parallels.

All of a sudden, Jack had a feeling that he had unfairly imposed himself upon Lorena, and he was flushed with guilt and regrets. She was in the midst of the most heart-wrenching crisis in her life, and he had interceded with his own needs without regard to how she felt. "I'm sorry that I've interrupted your grieving process, Lorena. I've been selfish and thought only of myself. You deserved better than that."

"I'm a big girl, Jack, and if I had not wanted to be with you last night I could have refused and had you take me home. The fact that I did not refuse can hardly be your fault. I know that both of us have got more work to do before we're free to make rational decisions about where our lives are going. Remember, we had a similar discussion like this at Pearl Harbor. First we were friends, now we've become lovers, and as beautiful as that was I don't want it to interfere with our friendship. I'm not sure if I'm making myself clear...."

"What you're saying makes sense. Neither of us have both feet solidly on the ground. I thought I was doing well at Pearl Harbor. When I came home I was shattered by my lack of progress."

"That's a natural reaction, Jack. You had not faced reality until you came home where it exists in ways you were not prepared to cope with. I know, because I'm going through the same process," confessed Lorena in a low voice.

"It seems as if I'm living in darkness one minute and brilliant light the next. The darkness came first in the prison camp. I thought I had left it behind in the Philippines. Now I oscillate between the two extremes, and I'm almost out of my mind about what to do about it," confessed Jack.

Lorena reached across the table for his hands and clasped them in hers.

"I don't have any answers that will give you relief, Jack. Just hold onto your emotions and pray for guidance. I've never prayed so hard or so often as I have during the war. Many things in our lives are beyond our power to change. We've simply got to accept them and get on with life the best we can. I value our friendship and I'm glad you came by to see me."

"Where do we go from here, Lorena?" asked Jack, gazing into her blue-green eyes. "When I told you that I was falling in love with you I really meant it."

"I believe that you believe it, Jack, and I'm flattered to be the object of your affections. I don't want our friendship to be damaged by commitments neither of us are prepared to declare or to keep. We need more time, because time has a way of making things which, in the heat of passion, are not always true indicators of what the future should be. Don't be impatient with me. I respect and admire you, Jack Ross. You're kind, gentle, and generous, and I'm fortunate to have you as a friend. I must tell you honestly that I am not ready to tell you that I love you for all the reasons we've just been talking about. If and when I do tell you, it will be without reservation. Will you settle for a very special friendship?"

"Yes, I can settle for that, Lorena. You're right, neither of us are ready to make long-range commitments. Thanks for making that distinction clearer for us. Where did such a lovely lady get so much wisdom?" Jack asked calmly.

She answered without hesitation. "By observing human behavior under grotesque conditions in the wards and operating rooms where young men's lives are altered forever by steel projectiles against soft flesh."

Chapter Thirteen

"It must be a sobering and maturing task," said Jack, understanding the source of her insight. It had to have been a suffocating experience for her, and he agreed with the decision of her commanding officer; it was time to send her home. Lorena had been on the front lines for as long as he had been in prison. Without some relief she would have collapsed in a nervous breakdown.

"Do you want me to take you home?"

"I think it's for the best, Jack. This has been a pleasant interlude, but there are some issues I still need to work through, and I can only do that by myself," she explained.

"What are you using for an automobile? I didn't see any around your house."

"The small garage in town has our 1941 Studebaker Champion coupe. Bob and I purchased it new soon after we were married. It has been in storage ever since the war started. There are very few miles on it. The mechanic said that it needed a battery and a muffler. When they're finished with the work they'll bring it to me. I also have one of those VIP gasoline ration cards. I'll have transportation, but I don't plan to be traveling much."

"What about your family?"

"My mother and father died when I was a young girl. I grew up with my aunt and uncle in Buffalo. My uncle is a Navy lieutenant commander somewhere in the Pacific. He's the main reason I became a Naval Nurse instead of an Army Nurse. My aunt died just before the war started. I never had any brothers or sisters," she answered soberly.

"I'm sorry, Lorena. I'm an only child too. I'd say that the Navy was lucky to have you. Since you don't have your automobile yet, do you want to stop at a grocery store for some provisions?"

"I could use a few things unless I eat peanut butter sandwiches all day," she laughed. It was the first time he had heard her laugh. It was infectious, and he smiled at her. "If you don't mind stopping, it will give me a chance to restock the cupboard."

"I'll even carry your grocery bags for you," he smiled.

True to his promise, Jack carried the two grocery bags into the kitchen of her house. "Is there anything else I can do for you, Lorena? I can split wood or anything at all," he suggested.

"I'll be fine, Jack. Thanks for asking and thank you for caring. Good luck with the family visits. I understand how difficult they must be. I'll be thinking of you and will send a prayer to guide you. Good-bye, my dear friend, drive carefully," she said, putting her arms around him and laying her head against his chest.

"I'll take all the prayers I can get, Lorena," he said, kissing the top of her head. "I'm convinced that I would never have made it this far without you. Thanks for being there for me. I'll always remember you as an apparition from Heaven when I saw you that first time across the ward on the hospital ship. Promise that you'll call on me if there is anything I can do to help. I mean anything."

"I will, Jack, but I'm sure I'll be fine. Thanks for asking, now go before I lose control of my senses. I hate good-byes."

"So long, dear lady," said Jack, briefly kissing the soft lips she lifted to his.

"Until next time."

Jack drove out of Warrensburg with a lump in his throat. He stopped a mile or two outside of town to blow his nose and wipe the moist film covering his eyes. Saying good-bye was difficult. Each of them needed time and space to get their emotional house in order. He drew strength and determination from her calm and logical outlook on life. It would have been easy to turn around and go back, never to leave her again.

123

The first stop for Jack was at Burlington, Vermont, northeast of Warrensburg. He drove to Port Henry on the western shore of Lake Champlain and took a ferry to Burlington. The family visit went much like the first two in Maine, leaving him emotionally drained and exhausted. He continued one after another with four more family sessions, two in New Hampshire and two in Massachusetts. By the time he was finished, four days later, he was physically and emotionally drained and was anxious to get home for a rest. He ached in every bone in his body and wanted to lay down and sleep. Jack had been gone for a full week when he turned the faithful Nash into the familiar driveway.

It was almost midnight when he quietly let himself into his father's house and climbed the stairs to his old bedroom. Jack knew that he was in for a long night. His malaria was kicking him around again. The intense weakness he felt was the early stages of alternating hot flashes and cold chills. His teeth were beginning to chatter as he got undressed and crawled into his bed pulling more and more blankets over him. He braced himself all through the night. The high fever was beginning to get to him, and he was too weak to get out of bed, so he pounded hard against the wall to wake his father.

Shortly, his father came running into the room and turned on the bedside lamp. He saw Jack coiled into a tight ball in the fetal position, shivering and shaking so much that his teeth rattled.

"My God, Jack, what's wrong?"

"Malaria, Dad. In my suitcase on the chair," Jack pointed across the room. "There's a bottle of quinine. Get it for me with a cold glass of water..."

Pops Ross ripped open the suitcase and found the quinine bottle. He checked the side for directions and ran into the nearby bathroom for a glass of water.

"Here, Son, let me help you sit up so that you can take some medicine. Then I'm going downstairs to call the doctor."

Jack did not have enough strength to object. The local doctor had delivered Jack when his mother died. He arrived within the hour, confirming Jack's diagnosis and told him that all that could be done was continue with the quinine, keep him comfortable and watch his temperature closely. Jack had the malignant form of malaria which produced high fevers, delirium and occasionally comas. The doctor suggested that if Jack got any worse, he should call and have him transported to a hospital.

A light blue tinge began to creep into Jack's complexion. He was covered with perspiration and continued to shiver spasmodically. At times he lapsed into a delirious state. Pops Ross was becoming more frightened by the minute after the doctor left. He should probably call the hospital. Then he recalled that Jack had told him about a nurse, an Ensign Kelly, who helped him. She was the one who wrote him a letter. Pops Ross feverishly checked Jack's pants and uniform jacket for the letter. He found the slip of paper Jack had written her number on at his hotel room. Without hesitation, his father called the number.

"Hello," answered Lorena.

"Is this Ensign Kelly?" asked Pops.

"Yes, who's calling, please?" Lorena asked, unable to place the voice on the line.

"This is Jack Ross's father. I'm calling to see if you can help me."

"Is anything wrong, Mister Ross?" she demanded sharply.

"Yes, Jack is sick with malaria, and I'm not sure if I'm doing the right things. The local doctor told me that I could increase his quinine dosage over that recommended on the bottle. It has been a few hours and it doesn't seem to help much. Do you have any suggestions? I know that you have more experience with the disease than the doctor."

"You're doing the right things, Mister Ross. You could call your local doctor to have him prescribe a new variation of the quinine you already have. It's called Chloroquinine. I'm in Warrensburg, New York, as you know. Jack and I are friends. I'm willing to drive to Wells to help you care for your son. Malaria attacks take a while, and he is going to need a lot of care."

"Oh, Miss Kelly, I hesitate to ask you to drive that far, with gas being rationed the way it is."

"I have a VIP card similar to the one Jack was issued. It will give me all the fuel I need. Please, if you need me, I'll be glad to come and help," offered Lorena. "I can be there in about four hours. It will give me a chance to see the Maine coast which I understand is beautiful, and I would do anything for your son."

"I can't refuse you, young lady. I admit I'm scared for Jack. He's all I've got now."

"I'll be on my way within an hour. In the meantime, keep him comfortable and make him drink plenty of cold water, even if you have to force him. Don't bundle him too much in blankets. A normal sheet is sufficient even though he may ask for more. Our number one concern is to keep his temperature within safe limits. Continue to wipe his head and face with cool cloths. Don't use ice water-it's too much of a contrast. Now, you should rest as much as possible, Mister Ross; you sound tired. I'll see you within a few hours."

"Thank you. I feel better already. Drive with care, Ensign Kelly. I haven't told Jack that I've called you. I hope that he won't be angry."

"The important thing is that we get him well soon. You've done what any father would do for his son, and if you had not called me and he got worse, I'd be angry at you," Lorena explained calmly.

"You sound like a good friend. I'm glad for both of you," answered Pops, relieved that experienced assistance was on the way. In the exchange of a few words Lorena had managed to make him feel better about the crisis. He was experiencing Ensign Kelly's most memorable character trait.

Four and a half hours later, Lorena pulled her light green Studebaker coupe into the driveway and parked it beside Jack's Nash. She grabbed a valise from the seat and rushed to the front door. Jack's father ran downstairs to open the parlor door.

"I'm so grateful for your offer to help. I'm Isaac Ross, Jack's father."

"Hello, Mister Ross, I'm Lorena Kelly." He was impressed with her beauty. She wore a pair of dark green slacks and a white blouse. Her hair was pulled on top of her head and held with a couple of red hair pins. "I came as quickly as I could."

"Jack is upstairs. Please excuse the disorder of the house." Lorena smiled at him remembering that Jack had told her about his father's fetishness for order.

"I'm sure that it's neater than my own place, Mister Ross, but I'm not concerned about anything now except to get your son well again," she answered calmly.

They climbed the stairs together. Jack was lying in his childhood bed, covered with a clean sheet. The first thing she did was remove a thermometer from the black bag she carried and place it in Jack's mouth. Sweat beads collected on his forehead. She deftly wiped them away. Checking the thermometer, she told his father that it was 103 degrees, high enough to be concerned about. She requested a supply of bath towels and a large basin of cool water. She placed a wet towel under each of his arms, between his legs, around his head and neck, and over his chest and stomach cavity. She cut away his undershirt with a pair of scissors rather than take the time to remove it over his head. As soon as the towels warmed or started to dry she would remove and replace them with fresh cool ones. She was also able to coax several swallows of water down Jack's parched throat every few minutes or so. Jack's father was touched by her warm personality and confident professionalism.

Lorena maintained a vigil over Jack for forty-eight hours, changing the cooling towels countless times, and administering quinine on a regular basis. She had also brought along a supply she had left in her medical bag. In time, the medicine would work, but the fever had to be broken first. Jack remained delirious and did not recognize her.

Isaac Ross insisted that he take over after forty hours so that Lorena could take a rest in the guest room next to Jack's. He had supplied her with coffee and several cups of tea and a few sandwiches. She refused any heavy food, telling Pops Ross that she would eat later. Her ability to focus on what was needed to be done was reassuring to him. They didn't talk very much during the two day period, but words were not necessary. He

127

saw much in the golden-haired girl that he liked and admired. Her beauty was natural with no trace of vain posturing. She eventually gave in to his insistence that she rest, and slept soundly for ten hours!

While Lorena was sleeping, Myla stopped by the house with Roselyn. Myla wondered if everything was all right. She had met the doctor in town. He said that Jack was having another malaria attack. She noticed the green Studebaker with New York plates in the driveway as she approached the house. Pops met her in the parlor.

"We've been having quite a time, Myla," Pops Ross greeted her and told her about Lorena.

"How did this Lorena know about Jack's illness?" asked Myla pointedly.

"I called her. I remembered that Jack had received a letter from a nurse who had cared for him in the Pacific. I found her telephone number in his jacket and called to ask her if there was something more I could do. Doc Smith did not seem to be much up on these tropical diseases."

"I see, Pops. Do you think Roselyn should see Jack in his condition?" asked Myla.

"I believe it would be best for her not to see him. His fever has been raging now for two and a half days and he doesn't look very good."

"Is there anything I can do?"

"I've made up a list of groceries. Would you mind picking them up for me, Myla?"

"Of course," she said, relieved that she could do something. "I'll take Roselyn to her grandmother and return shortly with the groceries. Maybe I can spell you for a while."

"Thanks, Myla."

Myla returned as promised and placed the groceries away in the cupboards and refrigerator. She then hurried up the stairs to Jack's room. Pops Ross was with Jack. She was shocked to see Jack shivering beneath the sheets. Pops told her that they had been able to hold his temperature below 100 degrees with the cooling towels. It was possible for temperatures to soar above 110 degrees which can inflict permanent brain damage. He told

Myla that Lorena had mentioned that an enlarged spleen could be a side effect of over-heated attacks of malaria. He turned Jack's head so that he could take another drink of water through a straw. Myla, too, became concerned for Jack, and had a strong desire to do something positive for him.

"Why don't you take a break, Pops. You look tired. I'll take over for a while. School is over for the year, so I've got more time now. Please go and rest. You don't want to get over tired when Jack needs you more than ever."

"Okay, Myla. Call me if anything changes."

"I will."

Myla changed all of the towels on Jack, replacing them with cool ones, taking the water from the sink in the adjacent bathroom. Jack still did not recognize anyone around him, but he responded to the need to drink the cool water. It was refreshing to him. He had changed, she thought. She saw the deep-set eyes more clearly now. His flushed face with a two-day beard stubble was covered with sweat beads. She gently wiped it with a cool towel.

He must have suffered terribly, she thought. She ran her fingers through his silver-gray hair. The tears she had kept inside for a long time began to run down her cheeks. She thought of the empty years when she believed him dead, and she recalled the years of pleasant memories before he left for the war. How innocent they had been! The cruel war changed everybody's lives forever. Myla sat in the darkened room watching Jack's body shake from chills. She wept openly and prayed for his deliverance from harm.

Several hours later, Myla was sitting beside Jack, quietly dreaming of yesterday, when the lone figure of Lorena appeared in the doorway. She saw a woman sitting in the chair and assumed that it was Myla.

Chapter Fourteen

Myla had a feeling that she was not alone in the room and turned to see Lorena standing in the doorway. It was an awkward moment for each of them. They appraised each other from head to toe. Myla was the first to speak.

"You must be the nurse that Pops called Lorena. I'm Myla. I'm not too sure, but Jack's fever seems to be dropping."

"Yes, I'm Lorena Kelly. This is a strange way to meet. I was the nurse that first cared for Jack when the Rangers brought him out of the jungle."

"I'm glad that you came. Pops told me that you drove from New York State to get here."

"Yes," answered Lorena, taking a thermometer from her shirt pocket and placing it in Jack's mouth. "I think you're right, Myla. He doesn't seem to be as warm. Hopefully, we've broken the fever. That's good news."

"Tell me," asked Myla hesitantly. "How was Jack when you first saw him as he came from the prison camp?"

"There are some things better left unsaid," remarked Lorena, seeing the desperation and sadness in Myla's eyes.

"I can't imagine how bad it was. He has never said a thing to his father or to me," declared Myla.

"His condition after three and a half years of prison life was as close to death as a human being can come and still live."

"Oh no." cried Myla, holding her head in her hands.

"Yes. He was a walking skeleton with deep sunken eyes filled with pain and horror, and he was suffering from starvation and multiple tropical diseases. Jack weighed only seventy-eight pounds and was a very sick person. If you saw a change in him, it's because he will probably never be the same.

He was lucky though. Many died and some went mad and withdrew from the human race."

"He seems to have recovered very well."

"That's a charade, Myla. Inside he's as fragile as any man can be," Lorena stated firmly.

"Has he talked any about me?"

"Yes, he's talked a lot about you and your marriage. I won't divulge what he has shared with me," declared Lorena, honoring the friendship she shared with Jack. "The two of you have got to talk, Myla."

"What is there to say that has not already been said?" Myla replied, raising her voice. "First he starts the divorce papers, and now, you're here..."

"Of course he has, what other option did you offer him?" Lorena questioned, afraid that the conversation could turn into a shouting match, and she refused to be a part of such a confrontation. "Look, Myla, your ex-husband and I have become good friends. On my part it remains a strong friendship. You'll have to hear from Jack what his feelings are on the subject. I'm not your enemy, and I'm not in competition with you for your husband's favors."

Lorena paused to make eye contact with Myla and continued. "Don't forget you gave up on him first. He never gave up on you. That fact should not be forgotten. His actions are quite rational for the proud man that he is. I lost a husband two years ago in the skies over Germany. I'm not looking for a husband. Pops Ross called me and asked for my help. I accepted the offer and would do anything for Jack. That's what friends are for."

"I'm sorry that I prejudged you, Lorena. I've been so sheltered from the real ravages of the war. I failed Jack, I can admit that now, and I'd do anything to take it back, but I don't know how."

"It looks to me as though the two of you have got to develop better lines of communication. Your daughter is an important factor, also. If I had a daughter like her, nothing would stop me from fighting for the man I loved and had a child with. Promises made are intended to be kept. You made a promise to Jack before you made one to your new husband, whomever he is. If I've hurt or offended you in any way, I'm sorry. I'm going downstairs for a cup of coffee. Pops is brewing a pot, and I can smell it."

"I'm not offended, Lorena. Thanks for the straight talk."

"If Jack's fever has really started to come down, he won't need me around any longer. I don't want to be an intruder. I want to leave the way I came, as a friend. If by chance you object to my being here, I apologize, but that would not have prevented me from coming if I was needed."

"I don't object," replied Myla defensively. "I... I'm just a little jealous that I was not the one to take care of him in the first place, that's all."

"Jack is hanging on to sanity by a thread. He has fallen to the depths of despair and lost hope, no matter how normal he projects himself. He's looking for some way out of the morass. You have the power and the means to make that possible for him right now. I believe that our friendship has kept him from falling deeper into the pit. For that I'm thankful. You may not want to hear it, but I can tell you honestly that if and when the time ever comes that my friendship for Jack turns to love, and he is not married to you, I'll lay my claim on him in positive and unequivocal terms. I have not done that yet, but that doesn't mean it won't happen some time in the future. You may draw your own conclusions and act upon them as you desire, Myla. The time has come for some difficult decisions that have to be made. Jack deserves that from you."

Myla understood the words Lorena spoke with wisdom and truth, respecting her sense of honor and fair play.

"You speak with intensity and conviction," said Myla, flushed with the intimacy of the conversation. "I realize that I'm at a crossroads and have some difficult choices to make."

"The decisions you have to make are mild compared to the ones you imposed on Jack," said Lorena, turning to go downstairs where Pops Ross was brewing a fresh pot of coffee on the kitchen range. "That smells good, Mister Ross."

"Sit down, Lorena, it's almost ready. Myla brought in a few groceries when she came. How about a piece of homemade apple pie? A local lady makes several every day for the small grocery store in town."

"That sounds good. I like apple pie. Myla is with Jack. I believe that his fever is starting to break. We'll pray for it to continue."

"I don't know what I would have done without you, Miss Kelly," admitted Jack's father, pouring the coffee and serving two pieces of pie.

"You would have sent him to the nearest hospital. They would've done what we've been doing. Thanks for the coffee and pie. I wanted to speak to you about Jack. Myla should be a part of his recovery. I'm going to take a room somewhere at the beach. I'm willing to fit in during the evenings so that you and Myla can maintain a reasonably normal schedule."

"You don't have to leave. We have plenty of room here."

"Thanks, but I think it's for the best for everyone concerned, Mister Ross. I don't want to be an intruder. I'm sure that Myla will be more comfortable with me not around while she takes her shift caring for Jack."

"If that's what you want. I'm missing something here, Miss Kelly. Jack has started the divorce proceedings, and Myla seemed to go along with it. Has she changed her mind?"

"The conversation I've just had with her leads me to believe that she would be interested in discussing it with Jack. If they could find common ground, it would be the best solution for all concerned, especially little Roselyn, who deserves to have mom and dad together," said Lorena.

"Oh, yes, I've thought that all along."

"That leaves Jeff, Myla's husband," Lorena continued. "His displacement may be difficult but, all in all, it hurts fewer people than the way it has started to go."

Mister Ross saw the logic in it and his eyes lit up. He looked at Lorena. She smiled at him over her coffee cup. There was a wistful look in her eyes that saddened him. He liked her, she had substance and dignity. He had even entertained that something might be possible between her and Jack.

"I have just one question, young lady. Where does that leave you in the equation? If I've gone too far, I apologize for prying into private affairs that do not concern me."

"You're a perceptive man, Mister Ross. Your son is a lot like you. If Jack and Myla can find it in their hearts to forget some of the things that separated them and concentrate on the future and things that can unite them, then there is hope. Jack and I'll still be friends. I'm not looking for a husband. I haven't completely accepted the fact that my Robert is never coming home."

"How long has it been, Miss Kelly?"

"Two years. His Flying Fortress was shot down over Germany. I've never received any word about his burial place or if any of his remains were ever found."

"I'm sorry. Loss of a loved one is always difficult. A violent death is especially hard to reconcile. I never said much to Jack, but I lost a brother in the First War. I saw him simply disappear in an artillery barrage on our defense line. He took a direct hit. There was nothing left of him. Nothing! I haven't been able to get that image out of my mind, and it has been twenty-seven years. No one knows for certain what another person is going through, but I do understand the depth of your anxiety and sadness."

"Sometimes I feel like screaming and want to run away from everything," admitted Lorena, surprised that she shared some of her feelings with Mister Ross.

"Dear Lady, sometimes you have to do that no matter how irrational it may sound to others. I never married after Jack's mother died. There were offers over the years, but I could not do it."

"What a wonderful legacy for Jack and a tribute to his mother," answered Lorena.

"I suppose it was, but who is to say that it was the right thing?" questioned Mister Ross. "I lived a lot in the past. My advice to you, Miss Kelly, for whatever it's worth, is to not let the past rule your life. The past has already been determined, and it's impossible to change it. If I had it to do over again, I'd do it differently."

"Mr. Ross, you're a philosopher and a romantic. Your wife must have loved you dearly."

"She did, and I loved her, too."

"The pie is delicious," announced Lorena, changing the subject. "I'll leave my medicine bag here. You and Myla discuss schedules to care for Jack. I'll take the night one if you two agree. I'll let you know where I'm going to be staying, and you can call me after talking to Myla. I'm going back up to give him another check of vitals before I leave." She finished her pie and bounded up the stairs with a determined step.

Isaac Ross watched her go. She had been a positive influence on the household for the past three days. Within that time, he had looked forward to her calm and positive ways. The thought that she would soon be leaving saddened him. He would miss her.

Myla heard her climb the stairs and claimed: "He seems to be resting a little easier than an hour ago."

"I'm going to take his vitals again," Lorena told her. Everything seemed near normal which was a good sign that the fever had been broken. She lifted his eyelids and checked his pupils with her special light. She acknowledged that they were satisfactory.

"I think we're on the uphill climb, Myla. You brought good luck with you today. Mister Ross will discuss scheduling with you for the next few days. Work out what is most convenient for both of you." She recorded Jack's vital statistics on a chart she had prepared and placed them on the table beside the bed.

Myla saw the soft professional touch she had with Jack. Most men would find her attractive and desirable. She wondered what Jack really thought about the blonde nurse. "Thanks, Lorena. You might try the Atlantic House near the pavilion at Wells Beach. The rush of tourists won't start until a few days before the Fourth of July."

"I'll check them out, Myla. Good luck. We'll have Jack back on his feet in no time," Lorena told her and turned to walk downstairs.

An hour later, Lorena took a room with a view of the ocean at the Atlantic House and ate a big breakfast in the dining room.

Later, she stretched on the bed and watched the waves break upon themselves as the tide slowly rolled inward. She phoned Mister Ross to tell him where she was.

"I talked with Myla, and we've set up an approximate schedule. We can take eight-hour shifts. If you don't mind, you'll have 10:00 PM to 6:00 AM. Myla will take the morning shift until 2:00 PM, and I'll take the afternoon and evening one. What do you think?" asked Mister Ross.

"It sounds fine to me, Mister Ross. I'll be there sometime after nine to relieve you. Has Jack started talking yet?"

"Yes, he has. He and Myla have talked quite a bit. How do you like the beach?"

"It's beautiful. Tomorrow I plan to go sightseeing along the coast. I want to see the Nubble Light at York. An attendant here at the hotel has put black friction tape over the upper half of the headlights and taillights on my car. It's my first instance of driving during a blackout."

"We're used to it by now."

"I'll see you in a while."

"Thank you, Miss Kelly."

"Why don't you call me Lorena instead of Miss Kelly? It makes me feel like a young girl, and I'm not that young anymore."

"I'll be glad to call you Lorena. It's a pretty name, and it rolls off the tongue nicely. I have a feeling that you'll never be old, regardless of your chronological age."

"Mister Ross, you flatter me," she laughed as she hung up the phone.

Later, that night when Lorena checked on Jack's vital signs, he was sleeping soundly. His fever was completely gone. She checked to see if Myla had added anything to his chart. The last three temperature readings were lower than the one before. He had stopped shivering about eight hours ago. Jack heard her in the room and turned to see who it was. He recognized her. She rejoiced. The malaria attack had the potential of being lethal to him in his present state. Now that he was over the high fever stage, his chances of overcoming the disease were pretty good, provided he did not return to the tropics and become re-infected by the malaria-carrying-mosquitoes.

"Is that you, Lorena?" asked Jack in a weak voice. "Myla said that you would be along later in the evening. I hate to be such a bother."

Lorena asked him to drink more water and held a glass to his lips. "The more water you drink the quicker you're going to get better, Jack."

"I'd recognize your voice anytime," said Jack after a long drink.

"You close your eyes and rest, Jack. We'll have plenty of time to talk when you're stronger."

"How long have I been like this?"

"Four days."

"Who called you?"

"Your father called me."

"My father?"

"Yes," answered Lorena, wiping his brow again. "Now please lay back and try to rest. I'll be here with you."

Lorena placed her chair so that she could read by the lamp on the table beside the bed. She wanted to be in a position where she could see him and the lamp light would not shine on his face. She made herself comfortable and began reading a book she had purchased at the beach, *A Bell For Adano,* by John Hersey.

Midway through her eight hour shift, Jack woke to see Lorena reading. He asked for something to drink besides water. She went downstairs and got him a glass of orange juice and some ginger ale. A little later, he told her that he was hungry for something. She suggested ice cream, and he thought it would be refreshing. She went to the refrigerator again. She was happy. Hunger pains were a sure sign of improvement. His color was much improved. She fed him a dish of vanilla ice cream.

"That tastes good," said Jack. His eyes were still red and swollen from the fever. She wiped them often with a cool cloth. "Did you and Myla talk?"

"Yes," answered Lorena not wanting to get into any heavy discussion with him until he was much better. "She seems like a nice person. She's attractive and intelligent."

"What should I do, Lorena?" he pleaded. "Myla thinks we should try again."

"I can't answer that for you, Jack. Listen to your heart when you make the decision. Right now you're too weak to even be contemplating such a move. You close your eyes and stop thinking now. Be a good patient for us."

"Have you seen Roselyn?"

"No, Jack."

"She should have both parents, but..." Jack's speech became slurred. He closed his eyes and fell asleep.

Chapter Fifteen

Myla showed up at the house around six in the morning prepared to take her turn watching over Jack. He was resting soundly when she came. Lorena told her the fever had finally broken and that it would be all right to give Jack a bath. He could also start eating things that appealed to him like ice cream and soups and lots of fruit juices. Lorena also informed Myla that she would be leaving in another day as long as Jack continued to do well. She suggested that Myla insist that he check into any nearby military hospital for a thorough checkup as soon as he was strong enough to move about. Most have had more experience with malaria than the civilian facilities because the disease was widespread among the servicemen that served in the Pacific.

"You've been a wonderful help to all of us, Lorena. I've been thinking a lot about what we talked about last time. I'm prepared to have my marriage to Jeff annulled. He may not like it, but he'll have to accept it if Jack agrees with me," announced Myla, feeling good that she had arrived at a decision that would make everything right again.

"Congratulations, Myla. It'll be hard on Jeff, but there's so much good that can come of it. Jack needs stability in his life more than anything else, and so does Roselyn. Don't take Jack's determination to seek a divorce seriously. It was an act of frustration and the lack of hope for any reconciliation for the future. I'm glad for you," exclaimed Lorena, giving her a hug.

"I'm feeling relieved now that I've got a clear goal. You've helped a lot. I hope that you can find the happiness you deserve."

"I was blessed with a very special marriage. I wish the same for you and Jack. I'll always be his friend and hopefully, yours too. For the immediate future, I intend to remain in the Navy."

Jack began to stir. Lorena had already checked and recorded his vitals on the chart. "Well, I'll let you go to him, Myla. Today you'll find a stronger, more determined patient. I'll be back tonight which will be my last stint. Good luck."

"Good-bye, Lorena," Myla answered.

Jack called out in the partial darkness of the room: "Is that you, Lorena?"

"No, Jack, it's Myla. Lorena has gone to her hotel room. She was with you last night." Myla felt his forehead. It was warm but not hot.

"How long have I been like this, Myla?" Jack asked with a thick tongue.

"Almost four days."

"I've been thinking about the things you and I talked over."

"You should rest more. There's plenty of time to talk when you're stronger."

"I'm well enough to discuss things," he persisted. "Where do we go from here, Myla? What are you going to do about Jeff?" he asked, pulling himself to a sitting position in the bed.

"Do you remember the time we met at the cottage?" she asked, placing a couple of pillows under his head for support.

"Yes."

"Well, you never gave me a chance to tell you that Jeff volunteered to step out of the picture. He said it would be the best for everybody. You two were close friends for years, or have you forgotten that?"

"I haven't forgotten it. Why didn't you tell me then? Maybe I would have had different thoughts on the subject. Regardless of what Jeff wants, the real issue is what do you want to do, Myla? You can't have us both. Roselyn is an important factor, yet nothing will work unless you want it more than anything. If we do this only for Roselyn, it's the wrong reason."

"Lorena has helped me realize how you and I deserve a chance for happiness the way it used to be, if possible. As for me, I've wanted that ever since I learned that you were alive and eventually coming home." Myla leaned over and kissed him on the forehead. "You'll never know how badly I wanted to take you in my arms when I first saw you at the classroom."

"I wanted the same thing, too," replied Jack. "I'm willing to give it a try. I've had so many dreams of us being together in the cottage."

"My only reservation is something I have to ask you, Jack. Please don't be angry at me. Are you in love with Lorena?"

The question hit Jack where it hurt. He had been asking himself the same question, and Myla was entitled to an honest answer.

"It's a fair question, Myla. Let me say that she has been a good friend and probably saved me from going crazy like some of the men from the prison compound. When things were going badly for me here at home, I reached out for Lorena and believed that I was in love with her. It was not that hard, you know."

"I can understand that; she's beautiful and charming. Most men would be attracted to her."

"I told her that I loved her. She told me that it was a classic case of transference. Every patient under her care was in love with her. Her diagnosis is probably correct. If you and I can find it in our hearts to reclaim our marriage, I promise to faithfully love you."

"I can accept that, Jack. Now please lay back down and rest. You don't want to overdo on your first day free of a fever. Close your eyes and rest." She leaned over him and kissed both of his closed eyelids.

That evening, Lorena found Jack much stronger and more alert. His eyes were clearing up and had a new brightness. He had been eating well and drinking a lot of orange juice. She took his pulse, blood pressure and checked his heart and lungs with her stethoscope. The last thing she checked were his eyes.

"You're doing remarkably well, Jack. I'm proud of you. You've been a good patient. I'm leaving for New York in the morning. Myla and your father have your care under control."

"Do you know that Myla and I are going to give our marriage another try?" asked Jack, waiting for her reaction.

"Yes. I've seen it coming. Congratulations. You two have an opportunity to give Roselyn a good home that all of you deserve. Myla is a good person, and she loves you."

"Do you love me, Lorena?" asked Jack pointedly.

"I've told you how I felt, Jack. It doesn't really matter if I do or not. You should be thinking and planning your future around your family. There was a possibility that you and I might have had a chance if things were different. The thing that's important right now is that you and Myla have set a course of action that both of you are comfortable with. Rejoice in that achievement!"

"Can we still be friends?"

"I'll always be your friend, Jack," she replied in a low voice.

"That means a lot to me."

"Now, on a lighter note, Major Ross," declared Lorena, with an impish grin as she rummaged through her medical bag. "I've carried a cribbage board and a deck of cards with me all over the world. I've played with a lot of different people. The men from the prison compound told me that you were the unofficial champion cribbage player of the camp. So, I challenge you to a few hands before you get too tired."

"So you're a cribbage expert, too," answered Jack. "We never talked about it before. If you're challenging me to a contest, there has to be something worthwhile for a friendly wager. What do you suggest?"

"How about a dollar a point?"

"That's pretty steep, Ensign Kelly. Would you pass me my wallet on the stand?" Lorena handed his wallet to him. "Let's see, I've got forty dollars in cash. I'll need some money for gasoline in the Nash. I'll accept your challenge of a dollar a point up to a limit of thirty dollars."

"Sounds good to me. If you're as good as your buddies claim, you're not risking much," teased Lorena.

"How good are you anyway, Ensign Kelly?

"We'll see," she laughed with an impish glee. Jack had not seen this side of her and chuckled at her playfulness.

At the end of five hands, Lorena reached the sixty-first hole. Jack was behind fifteen points. She triumphantly held out her hand for fifteen dollars. He begrudgingly gave it to her.

"Are you up to another round, Major?"

"Sure, why not," he smiled. "What have I got to lose except fifteen dollars?"

"I really expected you to be more of a challenge. Now don't hold back and give it your best shot."

"I detect an element of sarcasm in that remark. It usually takes me a while to warm up, so be prepared to lose what you've gained, Ensign."

Another game was played in six hands. Jack was the first to peg the sixty-first hole this time. Lorena was behind ten points and she handed him a ten dollar bill. The next hand Jack again won with Lorena behind five points. She smugly returned five dollars to him.

"Now we're even," announced Lorena with defiance. "How about one more game for double the stakes?"

"You're on, Ensign. I told you it takes time to warm up. I have a reputation of working at my best under adverse conditions," he bragged aloud, winking at her.

At the end of the fifth hand Lorena placed her peg in the last hole and declared herself the victor. Jack lagged behind her by twenty two points. He reluctantly reached into his wallet and gave her the forty dollars.

"I have a distinct feeling that you've played more than me, Ensign. You do play a mean cribbage hand."

She took the money and gave him back a ten dollar bill. "We agreed on a limit of thirty dollars. I would not feel right if I thought I cleaned you out of all of your money."

"Thanks for your generosity, Ensign. I'll remember this for a long time."

"You're welcome. It was fun," she answered smugly. "Why don't we call it an evening, Jack. You must be tired. I'm going to give you another dose of quinine. I want to say good-bye and wish you and Myla best wishes. If you're sleeping when she comes to relieve me, I won't disturb your rest. Shortly thereafter, I'll be on my way back to New York."

"How does a friend say thank you for everything?"

"You already have. It was nice meeting Myla and your father. I'll think often of you and pray for the success of your reunion. Rest well, friend, it has been swell being with you. You have enriched our friendship more than you know." She leaned over Jack and kissed him on the lips, before turning out the light.

Jack slept the evening without waking and without moving about in his bed as he had previously. All of his vital signs were normal. He had passed a crisis. Lorena left the Ross household soon after Myla's arrival. She embraced Myla and Mister Ross, promising to keep in touch. She started the Studebaker coupe and slowly drove out of the driveway, turning left onto Route One. Tears filled her eyes and an empty feeling of being alone again clutched her heart.

Lorena drove the faithful Studebaker through the center of Wells Corner onto the road leading to Kennebunkport. Mister Ross had given her directions to the cottage on the rocky shore. The minute she was near the driveway she could feel that the cottage was nearby. She pulled into the driveway and turned off the ignition key. The small cape cod cottage wreaked of energy. Lorena walked around the cottage to the ocean view opposite the driveway. Large ragged granite rocks were being assaulted by the morning tide. The restless waves repeatedly threw themselves against the tattered formations lining the shore, breaking them up into small fragments that drained back to the sea where the cycle started all over again with renewed fury.

The rolling waves thundered in her ears and the rising mist caressed her warm flushed face with cool salty spray from the ocean deep. The wind blew her hair from her neck. It was refreshing. She had always loved the sea. It had an elusive attraction for her. The years she had spent on the hospital ship were difficult, but the beauty of the sunsets and sunrises at sea were beautiful beyond compare. They never failed to uplift her spirits and helped to compensate for all the heartache that existed in the wards.

Lorena lingered for a half hour mesmerized by the pounding surf against the shore. The cottage and its surroundings were warm and inviting. It was fitting for the Ross family. She envied the opportunity Myla and Jack had for happiness. Few things in life have more meaning than living in harmony with someone you love and who loves you in return. Lorena left the coast of Maine and returned to New York with a determination to build a new life for herself without regret. She would carry warm memories of her first visit to the Maine coast.

Later that same morning, Jack sat up in bed eating a hearty breakfast of oatmeal and toast. He was steadily improving and getting stronger hourly. Myla was sitting beside him drinking a cup of tea.

"It's nice to see you eating again," said Myla. "How long is your furlough, Jack?"

"It was originally for the summer months. I'm sure that I'll be getting revised orders to fill the vacancy in the new program at the Veteran's Administration."

"Have you given any thought to what you might be doing after the war?"

"I sure have, Myla," he announced with excitement. "The State of Maine has a vacancy for an engineer. I stopped in Augusta to talk to the chief engineer and they'll send me a proposal for my review. An expansion of the road system is anticipated. A super highway is going to be built from Kittery to Portland and other points north."

"That sounds good." Myla was pleased with his efforts to find civilian employment.

"The war can't last too much longer. I'll have to go to Washington for an orientation period."

"Does that mean that you'll be away until it ends?" asked Myla, disappointed with the news.

"I'm afraid it does. Don't feel bad, Myla. I'm sure that the Army will be discharging thousands of men as soon as they can after the war ends. I had given some thought to staying in and making a career of the Army, but the prospects of work for the State of Maine are too tempting to ignore. If I resign my commission I'm going to join the Reserves anyway to keep my hand in military affairs."

"This afternoon I'm going to the cottage to air it out and see that everything is ready for us to move back. Are you happy for that, Jack?"

"You know that I am, Myla. I've never wanted anything except to be with you in our little hideaway on the coast. I've always loved that spot because it was the place where I was the happiest. It became a haven of comfort for me over the years. Being with you again at the coast will be the answer to all my hopes and dreams."

"I moved out of the cottage because it was filled with too many memories for me. The apartment I have in town has been convenient to everything. My mother and your father are close by and have helped a lot with Roselyn."

"How long will it take Jeff to get the annulment, Myla?" asked Jack soberly.

"I haven't heard anything from him about it. I hope it's soon."

"If you don't mind, I'd like to wait until that is completed before we move back to the cottage," proposed Jack.

"If that's what you want. Jeff has already moved out of the apartment. He did that a couple of weeks ago."

"Why didn't you tell me earlier?" Jack was surprised at the news.

"I wanted to but it just never seemed right to do so."

"Was I that angry and unapproachable?" Jack asked. "Yes, you frightened me, Jack. It was not like you."

"You may find that there are a lot of things about me that have changed. Can you accept that, Myla?"

"Lorena warned me about that possibility," mused Myla. "No, I'm not worried about changes. We can never be what we once were. That's true of you and me, too."

"I know," replied Jack. "To be real honest, the thought of someone else living with you and sleeping with you has almost driven me crazy. I believe I've got it under control now. It's a touchy point though. Give me a little more time, Myla."

"I understand your point of view. I can only say that I'm sorry for all that has happened. Roselyn needs a real dad around, not a substitute one."

"Her daddy has got a lot of catching up to do. I wish I had known about her. It would have helped when everything looked so bleak."

"There's a high school alumni dance at the high school auditorium this month. Will you take me to it?" Myla requested excitedly.

"A high school reunion?" Jack asked. "I'd love to if that's what you want. Do you think there'll be much talk?"

"There already is. You know how these small towns can be. No matter what we do they'll talk anyway. If we go and show them that we're together again, it'll either make them talk even more or shut them up. I'm not going to let them rule my life."

"Sounds like the right attitude, Myla. If you'll accompany me, I'd be proud to escort you to the high school reunion dance. It'll be like old times."

Chapter Sixteen

A week after Lorena left Maine, Jack was strong enough to do some painting and landscape work around the cottage. Jeff had obtained the annulment of his union with Myla. He made the announcement one day when he spotted Jack sitting on the porch of his father's home.

"You know, Jack, I've loved Myla longer than you have. You just never knew about it. No matter what you think about what happened, Myla honored your memory for a long time. When I was discharged from the Navy, she was an old friend who helped me adjust. Making the transition to civilian life with this was not easy," Jeff admitted, holding up his artificial arm. He was a tall, rawboned Swede with unruly blond hair. Jack remembered him as a moderate easy-going friend that was always working at odd jobs to help support the large family of second-year immigrants.

"I always valued your friendship, Jeff."

"In case you're wondering, I was good to her. She refused to live in the cottage because it held too many memories for her. I went for the annulment because everyone expected it of me, not because I wanted to," cried Jeff.

"I'm sorry the way things turned out, Jeff. I don't hold anyone responsible. It's time now to start healing and look to the future," advised Jack. He was saddened that their friendship of twenty years had deteriorated. "I bear you no ill will and wish you all the best."

"I expected that of you, Jack," replied Jeff, overcome with emotion. "Somehow, it doesn't help much." He walked rapidly to his car and spun the wheels as he left the driveway.

Shortly after the annulment became official, Jack and Myla moved into the cottage and began cleaning and organizing it. They created a room for Roselyn from the old study and moved the desk that was in the study into a corner of the living room. Jack's father carried a load of well-seasoned hardwood firewood for the fireplace and stacked it next to the rear door. Even in the summertime a fire was inviting and warm, adding to the feeling of intimacy. Jack was especially fond of the fireplace and started a fire in it almost every evening if they were going to be at home.

The night of the alumni dance, Myla was dressed in a light teal green formal dress with a lace shawl over her shoulders. She was lovely and Jack was proud of her. He pinned an orchid on the veil before they left the cottage. He wore his best uniform with a Sam Brown belt. The two were an attractive couple. Jack's father offered to babysit Roselyn.

"You two sure look scrumptious. Now go to the dance and enjoy yourselves. Rose and I have this front under control." Pops Ross was pleased to see his son and his wife together again. He had worried that it would never be possible.

The dance held in the auditorium of the new high school building was filled with alumni, friends, and acquaintances from every age bracket. A few of the alumni were in uniform. Jack had thoroughly enjoyed his high school years. As a result, he had a comfortable connection to the school, the town, and the people that made up the small community. They were his kind of people. The refreshment concession stand was located on the ground floor of the building. Wells was a dry town, and alcoholic beverages were not allowed within the town buildings. It was common knowledge that those who wanted to take a drink carried their own private stock in small containers or flasks.

Much of Jack's appreciation was due to the encouragement and help of a middle-aged science and math teacher, Miss Walters. She was a spinster teacher of many years who made each class member a part of her broad circle of family. She was beloved by many and feared by all. She ruled her class with an iron hand and demanded maximum effort from every student.

No pupil was left out or left behind if she had anything to say about it. It was common knowledge that she was always there for any student that needed help. Jack was not an academic type student. He was too much of a pragmatist, yet Miss Walters had ignited a spark within him for mathematics. Algebra, geometry, trigonometry, and calculus were her subjects, and she beamed at his aptitude for figures. She had suggested that he try design engineering for a career. He held her in such high esteem that he did as she suggested.

Miss Walters usually spoke a few words at every alumni get-together. She loved the school and the students without exception. They were her family, and it grew larger with each passing year. Tall and matronly, she walked with a graceful gallop and spoke in a slow, precise down-east drawl. She had bright eyes and a ready smile, even when she was provoked. As a matter of fact, whenever she smiled from ear to ear, she was about ready to explode.

The current alumni association president, a lady from Jack's class, made a few announcements over the loud speaker system that traditionally let off strange squealing sounds. Jack chuckled to himself. Some things never change! The microphone was turned over to Miss Walters who slowly and methodically made her way to the center of the stage amidst whistles and much hand clapping. Jack dearly loved the lady with the iron will and heart of gold. She started every class with the words "first of all". Her glasses constantly crept down the bridge of her nose and she patiently pushed them back. It was a contest the glasses won every time.

"First of all," she began. Jack smiled at her. It felt good to be back in familiar surroundings. "It's nice to see so many familiar friends and former students. I recently spoke to one of my new students whose performance in algebra class is lackluster at best. I had the pleasure of teaching three of his older brothers over the years. The oldest one was the worst of the bunch. He never got his work in on time and failed most of the tests. The second one was an improvement over his older sibling, but not by much! The third one, was a teacher's dream student. He was sharp, alert, interested, and punctual with his homework and did well on tests. Now, the youngest of the four brothers, who will remain anonymous, has started the cycle all over again." The auditorium erupted with applause and cheers.

"On a more serious note, dear friends and students," continued the gray-haired teacher. "Many of the old familiar faces that graced our halls of learning are not here tonight. A select few are gone forever, and we are all the poorer from their loss and mourn their passing. Those that are still at the front are in our thoughts and prayers that soon the horrible battles that rage beyond the seas will cease and bring our loved ones home where they rightfully belong.

"I noticed one young man in the crowd. He wears his uniform with pride and confidence. We were saddened to learn that he had perished in the violent contests at the beginning of the war in the Philippines. How great is our joy that we later learned that he had been spared and is with us now. I know that he will be upset with me, but I wish that he would come forward to the microphone and say a few words to his many friends who have prayed for his return to us. Major Jack Ross, where are you?"

Jack raised his hand above the crowd. "Go ahead, Jack," Myla whispered in his ear. He slowly made his way through the crowded room to the center of the stage amid cheers and applause. He gave Miss Walters a warm hug and faced the audience.

"Dear friends, it's great to be home where I belong. I can honestly share with you that I never thought I'd see the town I grew up in and loved, or see the old familiar faces around me here tonight. I never dreamed that home was such a precious thing. As most of you know, I was a prisoner of war with the Japanese in the Philippines Islands for three and a half years. During that period of time all the things we normally take for granted were denied us. I'll never waste food again because friends of mine starved to death. I'll never turn my back on a friend in need, because I know from personal experience that all of us are in need of a helping hand at one time or another. I always took the simple liberties we have for granted. Believe

151

me, when they're taken away from you, they become priceless beyond words to describe.

"While I was in the prison compound, memories of happier days sustained me and gave me the courage and strength to survive. I thank all of you for those memories. We are more than a collection of people, we're a real family community and that collective spirit showered me with love and hope through many dark years. Now let's continue our celebration in memory of the alma mater that binds us all. Thank you and God Bless."

Jack turned to Miss Walters again and embraced her. Tears filled her eyes. "I've thought often of you, Jack Ross. You've made us all proud."

For the rest of the night Myla and Jack danced and laughed with friends. At about midnight, he told Myla that he was getting tired and wanted to leave the celebration. It looked as if it might continue for a long time. It had been an exciting evening and triggered a lot of pleasant memories for both of them. Myla sat close to him on the way back to the cottage.

"Are you happy, Myla?" Jack asked. "I want to make you happy like it used to be. That letter I've been expecting from the Maine Highway Department came in this morning. I have a job in the York County area whenever I'm ready to resign my commission."

"I'm glad to hear that, Jack," replied Myla. "I was afraid it might not be available if you stayed in the Army too long. I couldn't handle another separation."

Jack squeezed her hand. "It won't be long, Myla. There's still a war going on, and I don't want to leave the Army until it's over. They've already dropped two of those destructive atomic bombs on Hiroshima and Nagasaki. Hopefully they'll have some influence on the Japanese leaders to terminate the bloodshed."

The next morning, they slept late at the cottage. The night had been warm and the windows were opened to cool the cottage. Suddenly they heard automobile horns blasting up and down the coast. Church bells began to ring, and the local fire department sirens pierced the air. The minute he heard the sounds he knew what it meant. The Japanese had surrendered.

The two atomic bombs had caused a heavy loss of life, but more lives on both sides would have been spent if the United States had invaded Japan proper; thus, the bombs were a merciful tool that ultimately saved lives. Jack hugged and kissed Myla warmly.

"It's over, Myla. The guns are silent all over the world, and it can start rebuilding itself. Thank God for that."

"Now I know that you won't be leaving me for combat. I'm thankful for that blessing," sighed Myla, relieved of the prospect.

"I don't have to report back until the end of the month, but I'm going to leave early to see what I can do to advance the veteran's program. Thousands of soldiers will be heading home, and they need this new program," Jack told her. It was the first time that Myla had heard him talk about it.

"I wish you wouldn't," begged Myla. "I don't want to see you leave again."

"It's different this time, Myla. We have a goal in sight. We can't forget that I'm a commissioned officer and I have responsibilities. I'd like to do as much for the fighting men as possible before I resign. I feel that obligation strongly. A lot of good men died in the compound. I'd like to do something in their memory for the ones that survived. Does that make any sense?"

"I'm proud of you for thinking that way," conceded Myla.

Two days after V/J Day (August 14, 1945) Jack was packed and ready to leave for Washington, D.C. He had notified his commanding officer at Fort Belvoir of his decision to cut his furlough short. He was badly needed as expected. Myla drove him to the train station at Wells. It was a tearful parting. Jack held Roselyn in the passenger seat while Myla drove the Nash. Roselyn played with the ribbons on his uniform.

"Will you promise daddy that you'll be a big girl and take good care of mommy while he's away?" he asked, kissing her curly hair.

"If mommy will let me," Roselyn answered soberly. She didn't understand why her daddy had to leave them, but she could feel the tension in the room.

"Cheer up, Myla. It won't be long. Look at all the things we've got to be thankful for and look ahead to. There are a lot of families that have to face the future without loved ones. You already know how traumatizing that can be. My absence is temporary at best."

"I know, Jack," she said. "I'll miss you, that's all. It brings back memories of the last time we said good-bye right here on the same train platform. It was July 18, 1941."

"You're good with dates, Myla. Good-bye, Roselyn," Jack squeezed her hard and kissed her red cheeks. "Never forget that Daddy and Mommy love you very much."

"I love you too, Daddy."

The train was pulling into the station. Jack picked his suitcase out of the trunk of the Nash and passed Roselyn off to Myla.

"Good-bye, Sweetheart. I love you and will call as soon as I get my new address."

"Good-bye Darling, I love you too," replied Myla, holding Roselyn. She clung tightly to her mother, fearful of the pulsating steam locomotive.

Jack saw Myla and Roselyn standing on the platform and had the same ache in his heart as he did when he went off to war in the Philippines in 1941. Tense feelings of being alone again were with him for miles.

The U.S. Army that Jack returned to in 1945 was a different institution than the one he had originally joined in 1941. Now it was a victorious Army equipped with the finest weapons and supplies available on the planet. When war started, the nation was severely deficient in equipment and trained soldiers. In four years the military had reversed the situation in an unprecedented shift of productive capacity from civilian to military goods. The citizen soldiers who were being discharged by the thousands at the war's end had joined up in the beginning with a passion to defend the nation. The courage, determination, and valor of America's citizen-soldiers defeated two of the most powerful militaristic nations on the face of the earth in a relatively short period of time. Jack was proud to be part of such a legendary generation.

154

Fort Belvoir was bursting at its seams when Jack reported for duty. Soldiers were trading their khaki uniforms for civilian clothes with the same fervor they had joined the armed services at the beginning of the war. The legislation that came to be known as the G.I. Bill of Rights empowered every veteran with opportunities that were nonexistent a few years before. The veterans signed up for college and other institutions of higher learning by the thousands, seizing the opportunity to improve their lives. Their earnest maturity and appreciation for the chance of a lifetime turned America's campuses into a more serious and dedicated environment for learning than it had experienced before or since.

Jack attended an orientation course at Fort Belvoir and was immediately dispatched to Germany where the Veteran's Administration was in the process of establishing a satellite office to aid returning veterans to make the transition from military to civilian life. It was his responsibility to set up an office at Allied Headquarters in Germany. He brought with him a staff of trained people to administer the legislation and help inform the returning soldiers about the rights available to them.

The orders to Germany included Jack only. He was disappointed that he could not bring Myla and Roselyn with him, but there were no facilities available for dependents anywhere in Germany at that time. He had considered resigning his commission, but his loyalty to the Army was too strong. Helping the soldiers obtain something they had so rightfully earned on the field of battle gave Jack a feeling of achievement and pride. His resignation would have to wait.

Headquarters was set up in a small town near Stuttgart, Germany, where a large Army complex was being established. The base was like a small city. He ate at the Officers' Club every day. On the third day of his arrival, he entered the Club at dusk, hungry and exhausted from a grueling fourteen hour stretch of work at the office. The Club ran a twenty-four-hour buffet table that was usually well stocked with a variety of foods. He selected macaroni and cheese and green beans with a large slice of melon, and looked around for an empty seat. Parts of the dining room next to the lounge area were relatively dark.

He squinted his eyes to make sure; he thought he had seen Lorena in the darkest corner of the room. A woman in a Naval Nurse uniform sat with her back to him. An older Naval officer was sitting with her. He approached the table and stared with disbelief. It was Lorena.

She cried out to him: "My Lord, Jack. Where did you come from?"

"Lorena," he said, shocked to see her so far away from home. "I thought I recognized you. What a surprise."

"Please join us, Jack!" invited Lorena. "I'd like to introduce my dear uncle, Commander John Reams. Uncle, this is Major Jack Ross. I mentioned him to you earlier."

"I remember, Lorena. I'm glad to meet you, Major. Please sit and join us as Lorena suggested. We were just finishing our meals, but like the old Navy hands we are, we thought we'd give your Army coffee another chance." Commander Reams was a man in his early fifties with an effervescent personality that made Jack feel comfortable with him. He seemed genuinely glad to meet Jack.

"How does the Army coffee compare?" asked Jack with a grin. Lorena was radiantly beautiful in her uniform.

"My uncle would be diplomatic and say that it was about the same, but I can assure you it is not," she smiled.

"I'm afraid that my niece has a habit of speaking the truth, but seriously, Major, the coffee is not bad."

"It's nice to see you again, Jack. You look much better than the last time I saw you," said Lorena.

"I feel better, too. You look as lovely as ever. What brings you to Germany?"

"My uncle agreed to escort me here to Germany. Red Cross records indicate that the body of my husband was buried in a church cemetery when his plane crashed near Stuttgart. A German Luftwaffe officer handled the committal. We're going to visit the site tomorrow," she explained with a nervous anxiety.

"When Lorena was notified by the Red Cross, I requested permission to accompany her. Lorena tells me that you were on Bataan, Major."

156

"That's correct, Sir," answered Jack. "It was a difficult time, but I've come through the experience extremely well, thanks to Ensign Kelly. I never want to see another jungle as long as I live."

"I can appreciate your sentiments, Major," admitted Commander Reams. "I see that you have the macaroni and cheese. It's my favorite dish, and it was excellent."

"How are things going for you and Myla?" asked Lorena, looking into his eyes.

"Her marriage to Jeff was annulled, and we redid our vows. We moved into the cottage at the same time. I'm planning on resigning my commission some time, but I want to help get this Veteran's Administration program established first. I have an offer from the State of Maine Highway Department for a job whenever I'm available."

"What kind of work will you do, Major?" asked Commander Reams.

"I'm a civil engineer with a specialty in bridge design."

"Congratulations. I'm a forester. I work as a self-employed consultant to private forestland owners. I'm anxious to get back in the woods where I belong."

The three adults visited for an hour or so after Jack completed his meal. He made the trip to the dessert table twice for a piece of custard pie for him and Lorena. The commander stuck to his coffee. Lorena and her uncle were staying in the VIP hospitality center of the Army Base.

"Is there anything I can help you with?" asked Jack. "I'm not that familiar with the surrounding territories, but I know the captain in charge of the motor pool. He told me to ask him if I need any type of vehicle."

"I haven't made any arrangements for transportation," confessed Commander Reams. "Perhaps we should take Major Ross's offer of a vehicle."

"That would be one worry out of the way," said Lorena.

Jack went to the lounge area to use a phone. He called motor pool and reserved a sedan in his name for Lorena and her uncle. Five minutes later he returned to the table.

"An Army sedan with a driver will be at your disposal for the day. This is the number for you to call when you're ready to be picked up at your VIP quarters." Jack handed Lorena a slip of paper. "Ask for a Captain Morgan if you have any difficulty. He's an old acquaintance."

"Thanks, Major," said Commander Reams, pushing his chair from the table. "If you two will excuse me, I'm going to take a walk around the Base and light up a cigar. Lorena hates the smell of the things. It has been swell meeting you, Major Ross. "I'll see you back at quarters, Lorena."

"Thank you, Uncle," she waved as he walked out of the Officers' Club. "He's been wonderful to me."

"I have a full plate tomorrow, but I'll find the time if you need me," offered Jack. He had been watching Lorena all evening. There was a sad, forlorn look about her that touched him deeply. "I'd do anything for you, and you know it."

"I do, Jack. This is not a happy time for me. I'll be all right with my uncle. It was nice of you to reserve a vehicle for us. I understand it's about twenty miles from here. Thanks for your concern."

"I've never seen you as lovely as you are right now," Jack admitted truthfully.

Lorena suddenly burst into tears.

Chapter Seventeen

"What's the matter, Lorena? I'm sorry if I offended you," pleaded Jack, holding her hand. "Please..."

"I'm just apprehensive and saddened about tomorrow. I should turn in. It's getting late. I apologize, Jack. I didn't mean to carry on like this in front of you."

"May I escort you back to your quarters?"

"If you want."

Lorena accepted his arm as they walked towards the hospitality center, a large private home taken over by the military. The evening was overcast and cool.

"Are you warm enough, Lorena?" She was dressed in a blouse with a light tunic-like jacket and a blue cape that hung over her shoulders. She drew long looks from passing soldiers.

"I'm fine, Jack," she answered, clinging to his arm.

"You're the last person I expected to see in Germany," Jack acknowledged. "I hope you can find some comfort and resolution in the fact that your husband was given a Christian burial. My thoughts and prayers will be with you tomorrow. How long are you staying?"

"We'll be returning to New York the next day. My uncle is the commander of a destroyer in dry-dock at the New York Naval Yard for repair work. It's almost ready for patrol in the North Atlantic."

"It has been great seeing you again. Here we are at your quarters. Rest well and good luck, old friend."

"Thank you, Jack. I've enjoyed the evening. Say 'hi' to your father and Myla for me. Take care of yourself. Goodnight."

"I will and you do the same. Goodnight, Lorena." He released her arm and held her hands in his. They looked in each other's eyes and saw a reflection of their own image.

Lorena squeezed his hands, kissed him on the cheek and ran quickly into the building. Tears were streaming down her face as Jack stood motionless watching her disappear behind the heavy doors. He stared for a long time at the dark entrance filled with conflicting emotions that shattered his sense of well-being. He felt guilty. He had an urge to run after Lorena and take her in his arms. The feelings left him confused and angry at himself. He had violated the spirit of the commitment that he and Myla had vowed again to keep. A simple visit of less than two hours had shattered a world he had worked so hard to create.

The next day, Jack was busy at the Veteran Administration Center. He worked feverishly for hours solving one problem after another. He liked the work because he was helping those men who had laid their lives on the line. They deserved every benefit the law allowed. Sometimes he bent the letter of the law to fit unusual situations and boldly placed his signature to the applications to show his willingness to accept responsibility.

The Officers' Club was busy as usual when Jack arrived. He lingered after finishing his meal. Lenora and her uncle failed to show up. Jack left the Club and went to the hospitality center where a worker on the desk told him that they had left to catch a military flight earlier that afternoon. He was angry at himself for not coming around to see them off and concerned about his bothersome fickleness. How could he have similar feelings for two different women at the same time?

Six months later, Jack left Germany on a military transport heading for Boston. He had written a letter every day to Myla and called her on the weekends. She was not pleased with the prolonged tour of duty in Germany, especially when Jack had been insisting that it was only a temporary posting.

Myla was waiting for him at the train station with Roselyn. It was a happy reunion. Roselyn had grown taller. Myla drove the Nash while Jack held Roselyn in his arms, amazed at the difference six months made in her.

"I'm back at school again," said Myla. "This year I have the sixth grade. Most of the kids are the same students I had in the fifth grade. How was Germany?"

"We did a lot of damage in some places. It's strange that the Russians seem to be almost as much of a threat to peace as the Germans had been," Jack replied, holding Roselyn close to his heart. "I can't believe how much you've grown, little girl. Daddy missed you."

"Mommy and I prayed for you every night at bedtime."

"I felt those prayers, and they helped me, Honey."

"You mentioned in one of your last letters that you might resign your commission soon. Have you given that any more thought?" asked Myla, concentrating on her driving. A fresh fall of snow had covered the road, making it slippery.

"I will, Myla. I wanted to check on the availability of an officer billet in the reserves. I'd like to keep the same rank if I can. Be patient with me. I don't like being away from home either."

"It's hard," confessed Myla. "Now that the war is over, it's time to find some normalcy in our everyday lives. The Army has had you enough. Are you sure that you want to be in the reserves?"

"The Army has been a way of life for me for a number of years. I'm anxious to take the engineering job with the state and will be glad to make that adjustment. However, I also want to maintain a certain level of readiness in military skills. You know, Myla, even if I retire my commission without joining the Reserves, I can be recalled into the Army if a national emergency develops. I'm subject to recall until I'm fifty-five years old."

"You mean they could order you back to active duty?"

"It would have to be some national crisis, but, yes, they would not hesitate to recall me and every other officer that has reverted to civilian status. Don't be angry at the system, Myla."

"It's still not fair."

"There's not much I can do about it," answered Jack firmly, closing the subject.

161

He felt a current of discontent with Myla that disturbed him. He knew that the strain of absence was difficult for her. He was relieved when she turned into the cottage and changed the conversation. The next day, Myla waved good-bye to Jack and Roselyn and left for school. He was looking forward to some time alone with his daughter.

He spent some time on the phone trying to locate a billet he could fill, and found one with a National Guard unit in Saco as an Executive Officer of an infantry battalion. He committed himself for the job over the phone and sat down to write a letter of resignation to the Army. He knew it would be immediately accepted. The Army was anxious to downscale its roster of regular officers as soon as possible.

By the time Myla returned to the cottage from school, Jack had made supper for them. He had shown Roselyn how to set the silverware, plates, and glasses on the table. She was an alert, quick learner, and Jack thoroughly enjoyed being with her. She was like a miniature adult. His love for her made him feel good all over.

"Tonight I've got some good news and some bad news for you," he announced happily, opening the door for Myla.

"What's the good news?" she asked with a grin.

"I've resigned my commission and have retained my rating of major in a unit at the Saco Armory. Also, I've accepted the engineering job with the State. I'll be assigned to the York County branch."

"That's wonderful, Jack," exclaimed Myla, giving him a hug and kiss. "Now, what's the bad news?"

"I've prepared supper. Beans and hot dogs are on the menu," he laughed.

"You're impossible," she scolded, hugging him again.

Life at the oceanside cottage was pleasant, as both Jack and Myla tried to seek the same level of intimacy and harmony they had experienced before the war started. Neither expected it to be easy, but they were hopeful that, in time, it could be obtained. Roselyn was happy having both of her parents. They went on picnics at the beach and took long walks along the rocky coastline. There was a small bridge over a tidal basin close to the cottage where Jack went flounder fishing often. The water flowed in and out with the tide and flounders could often be seen lying on the bottom of the riverbed, especially at low tide.

Roselyn frequently accompanied him to the bridge. One day she had a lot of fun trying to drop her line into the water directly on top of a flounder. The line had some clam bait on it and she positioned it close enough so that the flounder reached up and took the bait. Roselyn screamed with excitement and started to lift the fish out of the water. Jack helped her and placed the flapping fish in his fish bag. That night Roselyn ate her own fish and was proud as she could be. They had become buddies and were inseparable when he was not at work.

He frequently thought about where he had been and where he was going. Jack's search for place had been deceptive. All he ever wanted was for him and Myla to love each other the way it used to be. He had dreamed of soft passions and visions of loveliness that could turn the world into a wonderful place where he could feel that he belonged. At times he thought that he had achieved that dream. The opportunity to reconnect and pick up where they had left off was accepted with great expectation, and warm memories were often revisited. They did not talk about it, but each knew that the spark that had once defined their relationship with each other was missing. They rarely argued or disagreed. It was more like they were children playing house. The fact that the cottage was still more of a house than a home left each of them with a deep, inexplicable sense of failure. Something was not working!

Jack's obligatory two week summer training session with the National Guard began the first two weeks of July. It would be his first session with the infantry battalion. He left with the battalion for New Brunswick, Canada. Myla dropped him off at the Armory. She was distant and quiet when he kissed her good-bye. Roselyn watched her daddy climb into one of the heavy six-wheel-drive Army trucks. She liked the noise and excitement of watching the troops leave, sending her daddy a kiss as his truck passed by. Myla waved, but there was a frown on her face.

Two weeks later, the troops returned from their annual summer camp. Jack was looking for Myla and the Nash and did not see them. An hour later, when the base was almost empty, she still had not shown up. Jack was worrying that she may have had trouble with the Nash or had an accident on the road. Finally he saw his father's pickup truck turn into the Armory. Something had gone wrong!

"Where's Myla?" asked Jack, throwing his duffel bag into the back of the truck and climbing into the cab.

"Get in, Son," his father said in a calm voice. "I'm sorry I'm late. Myla didn't call me to pick you up until late this afternoon."

"Why, Dad? Has anything happened to her or Roselyn while I was away?" Jack was beginning to be alarmed.

"I don't know how to tell you without hurting you, Son," cried his father soberly. "Myla has moved out of the cottage. Roselyn is at her grandmother's. We…"

"What did you say? Myla has moved out?" Jack shouted.

"Yes."

"Why?" Jack could not comprehend what his father was telling him. "Why?"

"I don't know, Jack. Myla said she left a letter for you at the cottage."

"Take me there, Dad, as fast as this rig will go," he demanded angrily. "Why would she do this? I know that it was not like it had been in the beginning. We needed more than a few months to iron out all that's happened."

The ride to the cottage was long and painful. Jack leaped from the truck before his father brought it to a full stop in the driveway. He unlocked the front door and ran inside. A letter addressed to him was sitting on the kitchen table. All of her clothes in the closets and bureaus were removed. Jack was numbed with pain of rejection and cursed her as he ripped open the letter.

July 17, 1946

Dear Jack,

By the time you read this letter you will know from your father that I have moved out of the cottage. Our marriage is not working. You've seen that as well as I have. Assigning blame is not going to be helpful for either of us. I probably expected more than it was possible to achieve. From the beginning you were irritable and impatient when things did not go your way. You had changed.

Maybe we should blame the war. I don't know what else to say except that I'm saddened that the joy we might have shared was out of our reach. I admit honestly that my feelings for Jeff are still strong and I'm moving to Portland where I have the promise of a teaching job. I'm sorry, Jack. I wish it could have been different, but we tried. As hard as it is to accept such a decisive break in our lives, it could have been worse if we chose to continue. The level of happiness and harmony we both searched for evaded us. No matter what you may think, that is the truth.

Roselyn is at my mother's house right now. I haven't said anything to her. For the time being I think you may need her more than she needs you. Later, when our divorce becomes final, I'm agreeable to any settlement that is the best for Roselyn. You should bring her to the cottage as soon as possible. Her attachment and love for you is strong and deep. Tell her that I love her and will see her soon.

The Nash is at my mother's. The keys are in the ashtray on the dashboard. I apologize for contributing more hardship to your life. Maybe in time you'll be less angry with me and see that we were living a lie and that is not enough for either of us to build a future on. I don't hate you, Jack. I simply don't love you as much as I once did. Forgive me if you can,

Myla

Jack dropped the letter on the table and walked into the sitting room and stared at the ocean. A nervous twitch developed below his left eye. Tense neck muscles contracted to the breaking point, pulsating with every heartbeat. He didn't know what he was going to do or where to turn for answers. He collapsed on the couch and began weeping in long gasping breaths.

Twice in his lifetime Myla had rejected him. The sadness of the situation flooded through him. He never felt so insignificant and unworthy as he did at this moment of discovery. Slowly the pain and agony was being displaced by anger and an element of rationality. Myla's failure to continue the union they had recently reconstituted was not a reflection of failure on either side. Perhaps it was a recognition of truth!

Jack's father checked on him, placing comforting hands on his shoulders. "I'm sorry, Son. If I could remove this burden from you, I would. I have to say that I'm not surprised."

"What did you and Myla see that I didn't?"

"It wasn't any single thing, Jack. It was more of a feeling or perception that something was missing. Energetic passion and excitement were emotions I did not perceive in the union. The two of you went through the motions. I saw immediately that it was a far cry from what you two had before the war. It looked to me that you pulled the wagon, then she pulled the wagon, but neither of you got together to pull it at the same time. It's hard to explain, Son. I hoped that it would work, but…"

"Would you take me to get Roselyn?" Jack asked.

"Of course, the car is there too," his father answered with a deep sigh. It seemed to him that his beloved son was destined to suffer heartache after heartache. "For what it's worth, Son, it has been my experience that whenever a door is closed on us, another one is opened. We just need the faith and patience to look for it."

"Thanks, Dad, for always being there." Jack turned to hug his father. "It's strange, we never had arguments or strong disagreements. I know that my overseas duty bothered her. I guess I'll never know. Jeff must have been waiting in the wings to resume his position with her."

Three months after Myla left him, Jack received notice that the divorce was final. He and Myla were free of any commitment to each other. Jack retained title of the cottage. If and when it was ever sold she was entitled to half of its net value. Myla also agreed to fifty-fifty custody of Roselyn. Jack had insisted on that. They had tentatively agreed that Roselyn would spend the school year with Jack and vacations and holiday periods with Myla. Each were free to visit whenever mutually agreed upon. Jack had made arrangements for Roselyn to be cared for after school by her grandmother or his father, whichever was more convenient for all concerned. He also hired a neighbor, a young mother with two preschool children of her own, to look after Roselyn when he was at work. The arrangements worked well, and Roselyn seemed to be happy.

During evenings and on weekends Jack and Roselyn took long walks along the shore and went fishing frequently when the weather was good. She had erased the bitterness he harbored over the way Myla backed out of the marriage. Caring for Roselyn had given new meaning to his life. He needed to be needed. It would have been impossible for him to visualize a life without her.

One warm and sunny fall weekend, Jack placed a call to Lorena in Warrensburg. The phone rang several times. No one answered. He tried all through the weekend and still got no response. He called information for a Commander Reams in Buffalo and was told that there was no one listed by that name. His concern was sufficiently aroused that he decided to drive to her house to satisfy himself if she was there or not. Late Sunday afternoon Jack pulled the Nash into the familiar driveway at Lorena's home. A new Ford sedan was sitting in the yard. He cautioned Roselyn to stay in the Nash until he came for her.

Jack walked on the rear deck and knocked on the door. A tall elderly man with a light beard and a goatee answered the door.

"May I help you?" he asked."

"Excuse me, Sir," Jack nervously announced himself. "I'm Jack Ross and I'm looking for a Miss Lorena Kelly. She used to own this house."

"Yes, my wife and I purchased it from her last March. She was in the Navy then. She had her personal things moved out by a moving company and placed in storage. We never knew where. At the time we signed papers at the bank, I believe that she was at the Naval Hospital at Norfolk, Virginia. That's all I can tell you, Mr. Ross. We never personally met the lady. The realtor and banker handled everything."

"I understand, Sir. Thank you," replied Jack, returning to the Nash. He paused a moment to look at the ledge above the river. He could picture Lorena standing there watching the water below. The house and setting still had a warm, soft feeling. The fact that she was not there devastated him. Roselyn was expectantly waiting for him in the car. She knew something was wrong.

"Why are you so sad, Daddy?"

Chapter Eighteen

Three years and eight months later.

June 25, 1950, started out as a day like all the others. Roselyn was playing in a sand box her father and Grandpops had built for her on the ocean side of the cottage. Jack was working on a set of plans for a bridge spanning the Maine Turnpike. The stretch of road from Kittery to Portland had already been completed. The phone rang several times before Jack got to answer it.

"Hello."

"Hello, is this Major Ross?"

"Yes, who's calling?

"This is Major General Malloy. I could not locate your Battalion Commander, so am informing you as Executive Officer. I'm calling you from Headquarters in Augusta. We've just received a warning order to stand by and to alert all units."

"What's the occasion, General?"

"North Korea has invaded South Korea and is sweeping deep into the country."

"My God," cried Jack.

"The Far East area Commander, General MacArthur, has asked for more American troops. The United Nations are considering an ultimatum as we speak. We could be called to active duty. I wanted to make sure that you and your battalion are alerted in case this becomes a reality."

"I understand, Sir. I'll see that an alert is issued to every man shortly. How do you evaluate the situation, General?"

"It doesn't look good, Major. If we don't act quickly we could lose South Korea."

"I appreciate your calling. We'll be ready if needed."

"Good luck, Major. Your infantry battalion is one of the best trained in the state. You've done a superb job with it. If we have to mobilize, you can be assured that your battalion will be the vanguard out of Maine."

"We'll be ready, Sir. Thank you for calling."

Jack notified the commanding officers of the three companies in his battalion encouraging them to notify every man about the situation. His adrenaline was running high. They had been training diligently for such an emergency, and he was sure that the men would not let him down. Once he had set in motion the call to duty for the battalion, his thoughts turned to little Roselyn.

"Rose," he called to her through the open window. "Would you please come in here?

"All right, Daddy," she replied.

She was a happy, energetic child with a curiosity streak that tried his patience at times. Jack watched her run through the door. She never opened it and walked in; it was always at a run with the screen door slamming behind her. She had curly auburn hair like Myla. Her grandmother had cut it short slightly below her ears for the hot summer. Myla and Jeff normally took Roselyn for two or three weekends every month at their home in Portland. Jack and Myla had worked tirelessly to make her transition from household to household as seamless as possible. Jack was still bitter about the breakup, but kept it to himself. He and Myla communicated freely about Roselyn, adhering as closely as possible to the same schedules for bedtime, meals, etc., and reinforcing the same rules of behavior and conduct.

"Daddy has just received notice that maybe I will have to go away with the battalion if we're called to active duty. You've been with me to watch the men march and train. Well, we may be shipped overseas. We must be prepared in case that happens."

"Will people be killed where you go?"

"I'm afraid so, Honey, but don't worry about that," he said, taking her in his arms. "The lives of brave soldiers and grieving families is the price we have to pay for our freedom. We're fortunate that we do not have to defend our own land. One of your friends in the third grade, Fred Osborne, lost his father in the last war. His father was a good friend of mine when we were young."

"Show me where you would have to fight on the globe you bought me," requested Roselyn.

They walked into her room where he pointed out the Korean peninsula. "North Korea has invaded South Korea. The free world may have to band together to push the invaders back across the thirty-eighth parallel to their own country."

Roselyn studied the globe quietly and turned away, understanding the significance of what her father was telling her.

"Now, you and I should talk about what will happen if I have to leave. It will be for the best for you to stay with your mother. She'll let you see Grandpops and Grandmother whenever you desire."

"I don't like Jeff," Roselyn told her father. "He seems to avoid me when I'm around. Mommie scolds him for that. I'd rather stay with Grandpops. The last time I was at his house I promised to help him pile some firewood in the garage the next time I visit. He won't let me split the wood," said Roselyn matter-of-factly.

"I would hope not, Honey. You're a little young for that," added Jack. Roselyn's affection for her Grandpops was warmly reciprocated. Jack had never seen his father as relaxed and content with life as he was with Roselyn around him. "I'll call your mother and let her know about it."

The situation in Korea deteriorated and intensified quickly. It looked bad for the small inadequate forces that tried to block the powerful North Korean Army's march to the south. A few days after the warning orders were circulated, Jack received official orders to leave with his battalion by July 1st. They were immediately sent to Fort Devens where it went into a staging area to receive replacements and additional arms and equipment. They merged with two other infantry battalions from New Hampshire to form a new regiment.

The battalion then began a period of intense training exercises. He drove the men relentlessly hard and was resourceful and insistent that they were issued the best supplies and equipment available. It was all World War Two equipment. He was disappointed with the general status of readiness. It had happened at Bataan and it was happening now. It was déjà vu all over again. America's armed forces were unprepared for the roles the larger world community was asking of them. He was determined to push the men to the point where actual combat would be easy compared to training exercises. They were transported by rail to the Presidio in San Francisco. Once they drew their full equipment allotment, they were shipped to Korea.

Jack's battalion went ashore on August 20, 1950, at Pusan, the largest port at the southern tip of South Korea. They were rushed from the ship to the front lines where they took positions in a defensive posture around the port city. It was a last-ditch position of the United Nations forces. There was a distinct fear among the commanders that they might not be able to hold the line, and Pusan would become a Dunkirk-style of retreat to the sea like the British had to do in 1941 in France. Artillery fire from both sides had pulverized the rolling, hilly landscape. It was a war of attrition where very small gains or losses of real estate resulted in heavy casualties.

Jack's Battalion Commander was seriously wounded by a mortar round the first night they were on the line. Jack was promoted to Lieutenant Colonel and given command of the battalion. It had been supplemented by a platoon of heavy machine guns and mortars. The first thing Jack did upon taking command was to review their situation. He pulled one of the infantry platoons out of the line and placed them in half-tracks equipped with quad-fifty-caliber machine gun mounts. The platoon constituted his mobile reserve ready to strike at any point of the line that was threatened the most. He also relocated his heavy machine gun and mortar platoons so that they were at the two extremes of the line they were assigned to defend. They would be able to cover the full breadth of the front with their fields of fire.

Small arms fire erupted periodically up and down the line. Jack was a believer of commanding from the front, so he established his command post on the line where he knew what and where things were taking place. For two weeks they were an important component of the blocking positions that successfully saved Pusan from being overrun. They had taken heavy casualties while carrying out their missions. Jack had received a superficial wound on the side of his right cheek from a piece of shrapnel. He loaded it with sulfur powder and a medic bandaged it. The regiment was pulled from the line. When Jack's regimental commander saw the bandage he ordered him to the field dressing station in Pusan, where it could be adequately evaluated and taken care of. As soon as the battalion was secured at a staging area near the docks, Jack turned himself into a large medical complex under tents near the coast. A doctor cleaned and examined the wound. The antiseptic liquid used to sterilize it made Jack flinch.

"Ouch. That hurt more than the shrapnel that hit me, Doc," said Jack, holding a Thompson submachine gun on his lap.

"I'm sure it did, Colonel. You're lucky it hasn't been infected yet. I've got to assist at the operating tent next door. Stay put, Colonel, and I'll send in a nurse to dress your wound. Keep it covered and you'll be fine."

"Thanks, Doctor," replied Jack, sitting on a small stool.

A nurse entered the tent and walked to a medicine cabinet next to where Jack was sitting. "I'll be with you in a minute, soldier," the nurse announced.

Jack recognized the voice. He turned to see if he had heard correctly and looked into Lorena's blue-green eyes.

"My God," she cried, dropping a tray of supplies. Jack leaped to his feet and leaned the Thompson against a table.

"I can't believe it's you," he exclaimed, reaching out for her.

"Jack," she whispered in disbelief. Her face was flushed with emotion. She fell into his arms as if it was the most natural thing in the world. They held each other in a strong embrace. "How badly are you hurt?"

"It's just a flesh wound. Really a nuisance thing. My CO made me have it checked out. What are you doing at an Army center?"

"I'm assigned to the hospital ship anchored just off the coast of Pusan. Most patients are flown directly from here to Japan, so it's easier to initially treat them from a land base near the front. Half of the medical staff came ashore to join the Army," she said. Tears slowly ran down her cheeks.

"I was so glad to see you that last time in Germany. When you left without saying good-bye I was upset," said Jack, wiping a tear from her cheek. "I drove out to Warrensburg to check if you were gone. I spoke to the people that purchased the house from you. I haven't heard a word since. It was almost as if you never existed."

"I sold the house because I left the area. I had resigned from the Navy and worked at a private hospital near Niagara Falls. Please sit down, Jack. I'll look at your wound and dress it as soon as I pick up the stuff I dropped. I notice you've been promoted to Lieutenant Colonel."

"Here, let me help you," Jack said, kneeling down on the floor to pick up some of the supplies. "My CO was wounded, so I took over the battalion. We've been taken out of the defensive line temporarily. The scuttlebutt is that we're going to board ship for a trip around the peninsula for an amphibious operation. Nothing has been confirmed, but a lot of things point in that direction."

"I've heard some talk about that," she answered soberly. She covered the wound with antiseptic cream and bandaged it tightly with a strip of adhesive tape running across his upper lip under his nose. "I hate to do it, but the bandage will stay in place better if you can tolerate it. How does it feel?"

"I don't mind, Lorena. It's good to see you again. I've thought so much of you these past few years," said Jack.

"How's Myla doing?" she asked nervously, noticing that Jack was not wearing a wedding ring.

"She left me the summer of 1946. It's been four years now. Roselyn and I have had fun together. Myla and I share custody and try to make her moves as seamless as possible. It would have been hard without her. When I found that you had sold your house, my world fell apart, Lorena."

"I'm sorry for you. I didn't think Myla would do a thing like that. She seemed genuine and truthful."

"I can't answer any questions about her. I asked the same ones to myself. Roselyn is a wonderful little girl. She's made my life worthwhile. You know, Lorena… I never stopped lov…"

"Hush," she said, placing a finger to his lips. "Let's get this terrible war over with before we talk anymore. Your wound is dressed now. I'll give you a couple more to use every other day. Within a week's time it should be dried enough to be left uncovered. It's going to leave a scar on your cheek."

"I don't mind," answered Jack, hunching his shoulders in dismissal. He buttoned his shirt and grabbed the Thompson, slinging it over his shoulder.

"Be careful out there, soldier," she said softly in his ear. "You know that I'm assigned to the hospital ship, so maybe you can look me up sometime when you're not busy with your battalion. I'll pray for you, Colonel Ross." She kissed him warmly on the lips.

"I still have that same old feeling I had when I first spotted you on that hospital ship in the Philippines. You empower me every time I see you, Ensign Kelly. I'll take all the prayers I can get," said Jack. "Good-bye. I'll try to look you up. Now that I've found you, I'm never going to let you get away from me again."

"When this thing is over, you and I have got to talk," she promised, her voice trembling with emotion. Tears formed in her sad blue eyes. They kissed again.

"Please don't stop me this time, Lorena," pleaded Jack, reluctantly releasing her. "I've never stopped loving you. I know that it's not the time or place for important decisions to be made, but I have to know. Do you and I have a chance?"

Lorena's tears were unleashed. She shook her head in the affirmative and waved good-bye to him. He lifted the tent flap and disappeared, hating to leave, but buoyed by prospects for the future.

The amphibious assault envisaged by General MacArthur had the potential of bringing the war to an early conclusion. A powerful two-division-drive toward the South Korean capital city of Seoul from the port of Inchon would act as an anvil upon which the North Korean troops trapped in the southern part of the country would be driven simultaneously by United Nations forces from Pusan.

Jack's regiment boarded an attack destroyer a week after he saw Lorena. He didn't have time to visit her again. He walked along the deck of the destroyer in full pack with his faithful Thompson slung over his shoulder. He was looking for the hospital ship and spotted the large white vessel near the outlet of Pusan harbor. It was larger than any of the transport ships. He mentally acknowledged Lorena even though it was too far away to see who was on the decks. The ship had pulled anchor and was assembling for the Inchon invasion, following the fleet north to the western side of the Korean peninsula.

Once they got underway, Jack learned that his regiment was going to be the third regiment to go over the docks at Inchon. They replaced a Marine regiment that had not arrived in time. Jack's battalion was selected to be the point unit of the Army regiment and went ashore over the seawalls at Inchon. They immediately mated up with their trucks and half-tracks and plowed inland toward Seoul, twelve miles away. The plan was to envelope the city in a large pincer movement. The Marine regiments were sweeping north and west while the Army regiments did the same to the south of the city.

If the regiment ran into heavy resistance, the plan called for them to stop in place and call in artillery fire or air support to knock out the strongholds. Then they were ordered to proceed at all speed to get into assigned positions where they would take a blocking posture as part of the obstructing anvil. They proceeded in a single file with Jack at his command half-track being the third vehicle from the point. Few enemy strong points were able to stand up to the massive capacity of the four fifty-caliber machine guns in the half-tracks. It was an awesome infantry weapon.

Jack was ordered to secure a prominent hill south of the city. It would provide excellent artillery and aircraft spotting positions. His battalion was capable of capturing and defending it. A mile from their objective, the column ran into a heavy roadblock. Jack called in artillery fire and air support to insure that the blockage was cleared. The momentum of the column was maintained without any visible delay.

Gull-wing Corsairs and sleek silver Mustangs peppered the base of the mountain. As soon as they had dropped their bombs and napalm canisters, the planes laced the sheer sides of the hill with suppressive machine gun fire. It was an impressive display of skill and daring, and Jack radioed the pilots a "well done".

Opposition stiffened as Jack pulled the mobile forces into a semi-circle and dismounted his infantry companies. They assaulted the sides of the hill on foot. The North Koreans recognized the value of the hill as well as the Americans and defended it stubbornly. Jack led the charge up the hill going through a half dozen ammo clips for the Thompson. He signaled the men to remember the basic infantry technique of fire and movement and to keep as close to the heavy rolling artillery barrage as common sense dictated.

Jack was hit by a long burst from an enemy machine gun. The bullets stitched across his body stopping his forward motion, lifting him in the air. He toppled backward dropping his Thompson. A world of blackness enveloped him as he laid on the sandy soil in a pool of his own blood.

Chapter Nineteen

Jack could still hear the firing taking place around him. It sounded far away as if he was dreaming. He felt nauseous and light headed and went in and out of consciousness.

"Hurry!" screamed a medic to his associate. "Get out a syringe; he needs plasma quickly, or he's not going to make it."

The two medics stripped some of the clothing and equipment from Jack and drove a stake into the ground to hold a plasma bottle.

"He was a fighting fool," exclaimed one of the medics. "He was either crazy or one of the bravest men I've ever seen. He led the charge into the heaviest concentration of enemy fire. His pulse is weak; we're going to lose him if we don't get some plasma into him."

"I've got it ready."

A radio man stopped to see how badly Jack was hit. He called regiment for someone to take over the battalion and he called for stretcher bearers to get the colonel out of the combat zone. They arrived immediately and carried Jack down the hill to the nearest aid station, all the time holding the life-saving plasma bottle over his inert body. They deposited him at an aid tent where only the most desperate cases were handled.

Orderlies began to strip all of Jack's clothing from his body. It was saturated with blood. He had been hit by four large caliber bullets. One went through his lung and lodged against his ribs. Two bullets entered the chest cavity and exited the body creating relatively clean wounds, except that one bruised the spinal column exiting the chest cavity. The fourth bullet hit and destroyed the spleen. His heaviest bleeding came from the latter wound.

The surgeons opened his chest cavity and removed the bullet lodged in his ribs. They sutured off all of the veins and arteries that had been severed and connected the arteries together where the spleen had been smashed. They cleaned up the entry and exit routes of the bullets and sterilized the body cavity. Massive amounts of antiseptic and antibiotics were used to patch Jack's body and combat infection. The primary purpose of the initial surgery was to halt the profuse bleeding that had almost taken his life. If additional surgery was needed, it could be done at another facility away from the combat zone.

Jack was lucky to be alive. If it had not been for the courageous medics who treated him on the battlefield, he would have bled to death within minutes. Now, he had a chance. The bruise on his spinal column was an unknown entity. As soon as he came out of the aid tent he was placed on a helicopter and transported to the white hospital ship lying at anchor off Inchon. Once he arrived at the ship he was evaluated by a competent surgical team made up of several specialists. The surgical procedures he had received at the aid tent were deemed sufficient for the time being. Further exploratory surgery was not advised. Jack was placed in an intensive care unit where all of his body functions could be monitored twenty-four hours a day.

Lorena woke in the middle of the night in preparation for her shift. She showered, dressed, and ate a small breakfast at the nurse's wardroom before reporting for duty at the ship's intensive care unit. She casually reviewed the roster of patients, paying little attention to the names. Most of the patients were marines or soldiers.

Medication was frequently administered on a rigid schedule established for the individual patient. On each of the charts was a space for the surgeons to write their evaluation. Jack's noted: "Patient may be in extreme danger of internal infections especially in the lungs. Use of legs is in question??"

Lorena methodically checked each of the six patients in the room, taking temperatures and pulse and recording the figures. She wiped Jack's brow and paused, recognizing him instantly. She wanted to scream in protest that this couldn't be happening to him again. She felt weak and grabbed a stool for support. The room was revolving around her. Her assistant saw her sit down.

"Are you all right, Lorena?" the nurse asked, rushing to her. Lorena was losing consciousness. The nurse recognized the symptoms and quickly guided her to an empty cot. Lorena closed her eyes for several minutes. Tears seeped out from under the lids and ran down over her jaw.

The nurse was frightened for Lorena and pulled an emergency alarm. A doctor ran into the room and checked her pulse and listened to her heart. He passed smelling salts under her nose and watched for her reaction. Lorena opened her eyes recognizing the doctor and started to sit up in the cot.

"I'm sorry, Doctor, I must have passed out."

"The question is why, Ensign?"

"One of the patients, Colonel Ross, is a very close friend of mine," she answered in a wavering voice.

"Nurse," the doctor called to another nurse in the room. "Please call for help in ICU. Ensign Kelly is all through for the night."

"No!" protested Lorena vehemently. "Jack needs me now, not a stranger. I couldn't stay away knowing that he's here and badly hurt. Please, Doctor, please…"

The doctor smiled at her. "I understand, Ensign, but I want another nurse to help here anyway. You may stay and concentrate on Colonel Ross. Good luck to you. I can pass on some information about the colonel that will please you. His regimental commander is recommending him for a Medal of Honor. Evidently he rallied his men to take an enemy position that was holding up the whole regiment. Take good care of him, Ensign, I have a feeling he's a very special soldier."

"Yes, he is, Sir," answered Lorena, her eyes swelling with tears again. "A very special man…" She bent over him and kissed him on the forehead. "I'm going to take care of you, Colonel Ross. You're never going to be alone again."

Jack remained in a medicated state of unconsciousness for several days, being fed and medicated intravenously. On the third day after being hit, Jack's temperature rose dramatically. Internal infections were breaking out. The alert medical team began combating the fever with large doses of antibiotics. Lorena stayed at his side until she could no longer keep her eyes open. Twenty-four hours later, the antibiotics were working. The fever had peaked and was slowly retracting.

Jack was fortunate that the surgical procedures at the original aid station were carried out with skill and competence. Additional surgery was not required. He regained consciousness for a short period of time as soon as the fever was blunted. The first person he saw when he opened his eyes was Lorena looking down on him with a smile.

"Welcome aboard, Soldier."

Jack blinked his eyes a few times to see clearer. He heard the words she spoke and answered in a weak voice: "We've got to stop meeting this way, Ensign..." Seconds later, he succumbed to drowsiness and closed his eyes.

"Thank God," whispered Lorena.

Within a week Jack was strong enough to sit up and feed himself. Soups and liquids, especially ginger ale, tasted good to him. His internal injuries were responding well to treatment. That fact was a testament to the skill of the dedicated physicians that had saved his life. His chest cavity was sore when he moved or breathed hard. One of the bullets had broken three of his ribs and he would continue to experience discomfort until they healed. The lung puncture was also healing well. The drain tube the aid station had implanted was removed. He was responding favorably to every medical measure used on him, except his right leg.

The blow he sustained by one of the bullets did not sever any of the nerve vessels, instead it bruised the area causing it to swell. That placed pressure on the nerve tracks. The doctors were unanimous in thinking that as soon as the swelling was relaxed, the situation would correct itself. Lorena massaged his right leg several times a day to maintain muscular tone.

One day Jack asked Lorena about selling her house. "I'm surprised that you sold it. I had a terrible time when I drove there with Roselyn to make sure you were gone."

"Things changed for me that summer," replied Lorena, holding his arm while she took his pulse. "When I left Germany with my uncle, he suggested that I let the house go. Seeing Robert's grave in Stuttgart helped me to close that chapter in my life. The sale of the house was symbolic of that closure. It would have been impossible for me to continue and build a new life within the same walls that echoed with memories. I haven't regretted it. Life goes on."

"I'm glad for you. Where did you go?" asked Jack, anxious to learn all that he could about her life.

"I resigned my commission and took a job at a private hospital near Niagara Falls. It didn't work out well for me, so I moved to the Utica, New York, area where my aunt and uncle had moved after his retirement from the Navy as a rear Admiral. I lived with them for a while. When the war in Korea came along I joined up again."

"That's why I couldn't locate your uncle in Buffalo," mused Jack. "Say, I just got a letter from my dad. He sent along a couple of recent school pictures of Roselyn. She stays with him a lot. He loves it, and she's completely content to be with her Grandpops."

"He's a good man. His son is a lot like him," Lorena answered, taking the photos Jack handed to her. One showed Roselyn in front of the Wells Elementary School holding some books in her hands. "She's a sweetheart, Jack. She has your mouth and nose. How is Myla doing?"

"Myla and Jeff have two other children and seem to be happy. I'm not bitter anymore and wish them well," Jack replied.

Jack's progress was proceeding better than expected, and preparations were made to transport him from the hospital ship to a land-based recovery facility somewhere in the continental United States. Lorena told him one evening of the plans to move him to San Francisco via an overnight stay at Pearl Harbor. He suddenly became quiet and morose.

"It seems as if every time in my adult life when I'm beginning to feel good about myself, something comes up to change it."

"That's because you're getting better, Jack. It should be a time for rejoicing. The ship cannot hold all of the patients we get for an indefinite period of time," said Lorena in rebuttal.

"I understand that, and I gladly give up my bed to another soldier who needs it more than I. It's just that I'll be separated from you," he explained, looking into her eyes.

"I know, Jack," she said softly squeezing his hand. "I have a surprise for you. My Uncle has never asked for special privileges for himself in a long, distinguished career in the Navy. I've told him about your injuries, and he has been able to get me reassigned to a hospital in San Francisco. That is, if you don't mind being at a Navy Hospital instead of an Army one."

"I'll take anything to be with you, Lorena. I liked your uncle that short time I met him in Germany. Thank him for me. That was a swell thing for him to do."

"Do you know that the Defense Department wants you to get VIP treatment?"

"Me? What for?"

"It must be associated with the Medal of Honor that's been approved for you."

"A lot of men did more than I did, and they aren't getting any medals. I can think of a large number of worthy prisoners that died heroically in prison," reflected Jack soberly.

"I'm sure you can, Jack. However, when bravery is witnessed it should be acknowledged."

"Don't get me wrong. I'm humbled to be considered for the Medal of Honor, I'm just saddened that those who did more to earn it than I will never be recognized for their courage and valor. I'll accept it in their name if it's awarded me, and I'll wear it in memory of those who are no longer with us."

"I'm proud of you, Jack," said Lorena. "I'm sure that your mother would be proud of you."

Jack looked up at her and smiled. "I'm proud of you, too, Lorena, and I love you. What am I going to do about that?"

"One step at a time, Soldier," she returned his smile. "I have a suggestion. If you can be tolerant and patient for a while until we get back to American soil, I promise that at that time, we'll talk about the future."

"I can do that, Ensign!"

The competent staff on the hospital ship were in agreement on Jack's medical situation. His puncture wounds were healing without complications, and he was able to eat and drink most foods on a regular basis. They were quite certain that the nerve fibers that carried the electrical impulses from his brain to his right leg would slowly return to near normal as soon as the swollen tissue shrunk to normal size. Once the restriction was removed, impulses would be received by his leg. Before he left the ship, some feeling had already returned, and he was responding to minor stimuli. He was a lucky man. He and Lorena celebrated the encouraging signs.

Jack, Lorena, and several other patients were flown to Midway, Pearl Harbor and San Francisco in three long days of flying. They were assigned to a Veteran's Administration Hospital in San Francisco because Jack needed physical therapy facilities more than he needed medical care. The prognosis of the ship's staff was correct. By the time he arrived on American soil he was markedly improved. He could move his leg without difficulty.

A week later, a special ceremony was planned to award the MOH to Jack. President Truman was coming to California and approved the presentation ceremony at the Veteran's Administration Hospital. Jack was nervous about the president personally awarding him a medal. He didn't even have a uniform with him. Army headquarters at the Presidio Army Base took care of all the arrangements.

Jack's father and Roselyn were flown to San Francisco and put up at a hospitality center at the Presidio for the ceremony. Lorena met them at the lobby.

"It's nice to see you again," said Lorena, warmly embracing Mister Ross.

"I'm happy to see a familiar face, Lorena, or is it Ensign Kelly?" Jack's father asked, excited with the turn of events.

"It'll always be Lorena."

"You've never met my granddaughter Roselyn. This is the lady I told you about, Roselyn."

Roselyn stayed close to her Grandpops. She evaluated the lovely blonde lady in the nurse uniform that had just hugged him. Lorena kneeled down to Roselyn's level and held out her arms to her.

"I've heard a lot about you, young lady. Your daddy is going to be awarded a very special medal by the President of the United States. He'll be glad to see you and your Grandpops. I'll take you up to him, but first I wanted to meet you and maybe give you a hug. May I?"

Lorena's kind eyes and warm sincerity won Roselyn over. She ran into the outstretched arms. They embraced each other for a long time. It was a magical moment. A bond of trust was formed between the little auburn-haired girl and the lovely nurse who had cared for her daddy.

"Are you the lady my daddy went to New York to see, but wasn't there?"

"Yes I am, Roselyn," answered Lorena, her eyes moistening. "Come with me. I'll take you to the hospital where you can see your father. He was very badly wounded. He's still weak and in need of rest and therapy, but he's going to be fine. All the prayers that the two of you have been saying have been answered."

The next morning, Lorena was sitting beside Jack's bed waiting for him to wake up. He stirred slightly and opened his eyes, feeling that someone was watching him.

"Good morning, Jack," Lorena greeted, kissing him softly.

"My, what a nice way to start a morning."

"I told you that when we got to the United States you and I would have to talk. I'm sure that you want some clarification and direction as much as I want to give it to you."

"I'm not too sure what you're trying to say, Lorena, but..."

"Do you remember the time we met in Germany?"

"Yes."

"Well, I was three months pregnant then with your child. Remember Lake George?"

"I'm so sorry, Lorena," cried Jack.

"You have nothing to be sorry for, Jack. It was the most beautiful thing that has happened to me since the war started.

185

That was why I resigned my Navy commission and moved away from Warrensburg."

"Why didn't you tell me about your condition?"

"I thought you and Myla were still married. I had no way of knowing otherwise. It would have been devastating to your marriage, so I remained quiet."

Jack sat upright and pulled his legs over the side of the hospital bed. "Do you mean to tell me that you've gone through all of that, and I was not there with you to help?"

Lorena reached for an envelope on the bed stand.

"Here are some recent photographs of our son. He's living with my aunt and uncle near Utica."

Jack received the photos with shaking hands. He silently looked at them one by one, studying each one closely. He began to cry softly.

"He looks like me in some old pictures when I was a little boy. I can't believe I'm looking at my son. What's his name?"

"I named him David Jack Kelly after you and my dead father. He's a precious little boy and his mommy loves him dearly." Lorena began to cry. It was a powerful moment that they would remember for the rest of their lives.

"Will you marry me, Lorena?"

"Yes, I'll marry you, Jack. From this day on we face the future together. No more being alone and no more good-byes."

THE END

Other Historical Romance Novels
BY
Clifton LaBree

A Song for Lisa   A Historical Romance

This is the story of a young American woman captured by the Japanese in the Philippines, 1941. Like most prisoners, she was brutalized and sadistically treated with a cruel disregard for human life. Three years later, Lisa and her companions had reached the low point of starvation and abuse .....

Lake of Three Sorrows   A Historical Romance

A warm spiritually uplifting story of courage, commitment, and sacrifice. This is the story of Dale Cooper, a battle-weary American soldier who served in two world wars.

Flickering Flame (Colonial Series Book One)

A historical novel, about the Cullen family who settled in Portsmouth, New Hampshire, and their participation in events prior to the French and Indian War. Freedom and opportunity were on the march, but it extracted a heavy price. Frontier settlers were ruthlessly killed and butchered by rampaging Indians lead by French officers and Jesuit priests who frequently incited them to greater levels of inhumanity...

Raising the Torch (Colonial Series Book Two)

A continuation of the saga from Flickering Flame, Colonial Series book one, of the Cullen family in Colonial Portsmouth. This is a moving story of love and sacrifice when a small colony had the audacity to fight for independence from their motherland...

Non-Fiction Books

By

Clifton LaBree

New Hampshire's General John Stark, Live Free or Die: Death Is Not the Greatest of Evils

Publisher - Fading Shadows Imprint

A fresh look at one of America's staunchest defenders of liberty and freedom. John Stark was a courageous New Hampshire citizen-soldier who fought in both, the French and Indian War, and the Revolutionary War. His pursuit of leadership excellence on the battlefield distinguished him as one of the most successful combat commanders of the war, and one of the least appreciated.

His selflessness, modest life style, and devotion to the cause of freedom are an inspiration that time has not diminished. He remains today the embodiment of the frugal, independent, and cantankerous New Hampshire Yankee.

Gentle Warrior, General Oliver Prince Smith, USMC

Published by - Kent State University Press. Kent, Ohio, 2001

The Story of one of the United States Marine Corps best General Officer. His flawless performance in Korea is a story that needed to be told.

FADING SHADOWS IMPRINT

Fading Shadows Imprint was established to bring to the public books of historical events and portraits of people enduring tragic circumstances of by-gone days. Hopefully, they will generate a deep appreciation and respect for the exceptionalness of the United States of America, and an appreciation for the sacrifice and selflessness of those who valiantly served for liberty and freedom.

The characters are fictional, but the historical events and dates have been seriously researched and are factually presented. Some books feature incidents during the French and Indian Wars as well as the War for Independence.

World Wars I and II are eras rich in stories that beg to be told. I've tried to pay tribute to the collective courage and heroism, often unheralded, that has defined Americans in every engagement. It was a time when the immortality of dreams and aspirations were defended by the blood of young men and women. There is a beautiful monument and cemetery in a small French village where thousands of white crosses and Stars-of-David are set in perfect alignment, honoring thousands of American soldiers who gave their last full measure. A large granite slab bearing mute witness to their sacrifice has the following words chiseled in stone: TIME WILL NOT DIM THE GLORY OF THEIR DEEDS. Another monument reads: VIRTUE AND COURAGE ARE THEIR OWN MONUMENT AND REWARD. Those simple words define the American soldier from the dark days of the Revolutionary War to the present. They are an American treasure, unique in the history of the world.

Every generation has its own signature and characteristics that uniquely define them. The World War II generation is defined by the immortality of the ideals and truth they gallantly defended.

The United States has freely given precious blood and treasure to defend the rights of man to be free, and we have never asked for anything in return. No other nation on the planet has sacrificed so much for the noble virtues of liberty and freedom. We hope that the selections offered by Fading Shadows Imprint will touch your hearts and generate a deeper appreciation and love for our country.

www.ingramcontent.com/pod-product-compliance
Lightning Source LLC
Chambersburg PA
CBHW071312200626
46813CB00015B/1569